Breaking the Clouds

Breaking the Clouds

Margaret Blake

ROBERT HALE · LONDON

© Margaret Blake 2008
First published in Great Britain 2008

ISBN 978-0-7090-8562-1

Robert Hale Limited
Clerkenwell House
Clerkenwell Green
London EC1R 0HT

www.halebooks.com

2 4 6 8 10 9 7 5 3 1

Typeset in 11½/15½pt New Century Schoolbook
by Derek Doyle & Associates, Shaw Heath
Printed and bound in Great Britain
by Biddles Limited, King's Lynn

For John, Dan Alyce, Madeleine, Hayden and Spencer,
with all my love.

CHAPTER ONE

BRON was not sure when she realized that her life was spiralling out of control. She had been so happy and maybe that was a problem. Coming to live in New Zealand was a good move for her. She had a good job – deputy head at a small school – and a beautiful home, far grander than she could afford to buy in England. Most importantly she loved the country. Not only were the people friendly and gracious, but she could do all the things she loved, sailing in particular.

No, the problem was not with her but with her husband, Jack. It had been his idea to come to North Island, New Zealand; she had not been bothered but since her parents had been killed, there was nothing to really keep her in England and she had always been adventurous anyway.

Ducks to water came to mind: that was how she had taken to the country. Jack, however, had massive problems. He hated it. That he had not given it a real chance was clear but she was sympathetic to his homesickness, if indeed that was what it was. He never actually said that was the problem.

He chafed at life in the far north and had left his position as a lawyer in a country practice and moved to Auckland. 'You stay up here – it might not work out for me down there,' he had said.

It was not ideal but she had gone along with it. After all, they had so much invested where they were living. It was hardly likely that she would be able to get such a good job if she moved to the city.

At first it was OK. Jack came home at weekends and they went sailing but then he started missing weekends. When he came home he drank more than she had ever noticed before. When she suggested he go back to England for a holiday, let him see what he was missing, he said the idea was ridiculous. Besides, he had to get established in his new firm.

'But if you are unhappy. . . .'

'Oh, shut up, Bron, I don't want to talk about it. You're such a nag these days.'

Taking out the boat and then swimming off Russell had done nothing for her worries.

She had thought it would take her mind off her problems but the peace and quiet just blew them right back in her face.

As she nudged the boat into its berth, alongside the motor-sailer, she barely noticed the man on the pontoon.

'Wake up there!'

'Sorry.'

'Throw me the line, Bron.'

She did so and the man caught it smoothly, fastening it around a bollard.

'How you doing?' he asked with a grin.

'I'm fine.'

'Fancy a coffee? I have some freshly made.'

'Sounds good.' She really wanted to be alone to mull over things, yet that seemed unfriendly and, anyway, she liked the bloke.

She scrambled from her boat on to his. There was a delicious aroma of fresh coffee. Taking a seat on deck, she waited for him to bring it from below.

She really liked Job Tepi: he was the brother of her closest neighbour Ruthie and had his sister's easygoing, friendly charm.

The Tepi clan were the product of a union between a Scottish great-grandmother and a Maori great-grandfather. Job was too good-looking for his own good, she often thought. He had thick jet black hair that he wore long and tied back with an elastic band. His skin was like highly polished copper and his body was slim but muscled. He owned two successful hotels. It was hard to believe, looking at him, that he was quite a businessman. He generally went around dressed in denim shorts and T-shirts. Only once had she seen him 'dressed up' and that had been at his sister's Burns Night party last year.

'You looked miles away,' he said. 'School's out – can't be worried about that.'

'No.' She blushed. Job was too easy to talk to; she had had coffee with him before and something about him teased things out of her. She definitely did not want to discuss her marital problems with him – *him of all people!*

'To tell you the truth . . . I am a bit bothered about a letter I got today.'

'Oh, really?'

His eyes were very dark but there were tiny slivers of green against the black irises. There seemed to be something in there, something more than curiosity. Surely not fear? She was being ridiculous. Why would he be afraid of any letter she would receive? Was she getting paranoid as well as worried?

'From a cousin. Marged. She's going to come over here.'

'And that is bad news because. . . ?'

'I didn't say it was bad news.'

'You said you were worried.'

'Well, yes . . . no, I . . . it sounds terrible but, well she and I don't exactly get on.'

'What's terrible about that, Bron? Thank God for friends, don't you say that? I have plenty of relations that I would not give houseroom to. It's not a problem.'

'You have dozens of relations. I have only her and her mother. I was an only child, my mam had one brother and my father was an only child. We're a tiny family, not even a family proper. Marged is a strange girl. Not her fault. She was always under the thumb of her mother. They went everywhere together, and I mean everywhere, even when she was a teenager. She never went to dances or clubs. I don't think she ever went in a pub with her mates.'

'Wow, strange,' he conceded.

'Her mother was horrendous, really possessive. My mam put up with her because she was her brother's wife, and then when he died, well, mam felt she had to keep the family together. My mam was full of love and personality. A real chatty Welsh girl. How she tolerated those two introverts I'll never know.'

'And now she wants to come, with her mother?'

'No, she said she's coming on her own. That is odd. I mean, Marged getting away from her mother is like someone successfully breaking out of Alcatraz.'

Job laughed softly. Bron did not want to go on talking about Marged, but it was at least better than telling this man about Jack.

'The strangest thing, though, is that Marged once married. I don't know how she met this guy, though they did have a sweets and tobacco shop so he could've been a customer, but how they courted I'll never know. Anyway, when they did marry he went to live with them. It was a sort of really weird ménage a trois. It didn't last. He went away. He was a good-looking lad too, dark and attractive, sort of Italian-looking. I think my aunt must have driven him away.'

'Sounds to me like Marged had a sad life,' he said.

These words made her feel guilty. Yet how could she explain how she felt about Marged? How things seemed to happen when she was around. Bron always seemed to lose things, or things got ruined when she was visiting. Bron was always the one to be blamed. Pure innocent Marged, fair and beautiful with her long blonde plait of hair, could never do anything wrong.

'She did. I am totally selfish but things . . .' She stopped biting off the words, dredging her mind for something to say. 'Well, things will be OK, I'm off school as you said. It will be fine.'

'When she's coming?'

'Tomorrow. I have to meet her at the airport. It's not a problem!'

Oh, but it is, she thought. With Jack how he is, it's going to make for a tense situation.

'Well, if I can do anything. You know, take her sailing, or we have things at the hotel she could join in with. There are a couple of day trips we do. Just give me a ring, it won't be a problem.'

'Thank you, Job, that's thoughtful of you.'

'I'm a thoughtful kind of fellow.'

Bron forced a smile and watched her cousin approach. Marged was different and yet the same. She had maturity about her and although she still had the long, fair plait, it was now doubled at the nape of her neck. It should have

11

made her look like a nineteenth-century spinster school teacher, but there was a hint of sensuality about her round face and full lips that battered that image into the ground.

She was wearing a dark blue business suit and crisp white blouse. Hardly the stuff for flying to the other side of the world in, not if you were after comfort, Bron thought. But again, Marged looked perfectly comfortable. She must have caught something in Bron's eye for she said, 'I thought dressed like this I'd get an upgrade and I did . . . from Los Angeles to here.'

'Excellent. I travel like a slob in a tracksuit,' Bron admitted, 'and I've never had an upgrade yet. I guess I've learned something today.'

Marged smiled, a full-lipped smile hiding her teeth, as she leaned forward and hugged her cousin. She had never been affectionate so it took Bron a moment to respond to this new Marged and a frisson of alarm travelled down her spine. She shook it off as being ridiculous. She was so sensitive to things these days.

'You must be exhausted, upgrade or not.'

'A little but I must keep to New Zealand time. At least, that was what the man sitting next to me advised.'

'He's right, you should, but it will be difficult. Come on, let me take your bag. Just one suitcase – I am impressed.'

'I intend to shop while I am here. I haven't any decent summer clothes. Someone at work said clothes were quite cheap here.'

'Well, yes, they can be. It's a long drive to our house, Marged; I hope you'll be OK.'

'I'll be fine. Don't worry about me, Bron.'

Bron would have preferred Jack to come with her but he claimed he had appointments with clients. It would have been preferable to perhaps have stayed in Auckland overnight but again Jack had said it wasn't necessary and anyway, it just might mess Marged up and tempt her to go to bed too early. She accepted what he said, just as she was trying to accept her changed husband. The man she had married had been warm and sensitive, but now. . . .

The traffic wasn't too bad and soon they had left the city behind. Marged chatted, more than Bron could remember her ever doing. She had been a fairly silent little girl. The scenery took her attention for a while then Bron remembered something and asked, 'How is your mother, Marged?'

Marged gave a little gasp.

'Are you OK?'

'But you must know, Bronwen,' she said desperately.

'Know what? Look, Marged, you just asked if you could come. You didn't tell me anything was wrong. Is something wrong?'

'You could say that,' she said quietly, then very coldly added, 'My mother is dead.'

'Oh, Marged, *I am so sorry*!' Up ahead was a small roadside café. Bron steered the car into the parking lot. 'Let's have a coffee. . . .'

'I was sure I had written to you – are you certain you did not get a letter?' Marged asked her question in a tone that showed her disbelief.

'I never received a letter,' Bron said. 'Did you not wonder why I hadn't written to you? I would have written or telephoned. Surely that made you suspicious.' Marged did not reply for a while and then said sulkily, 'I suppose so, but I didn't think about it. I was feeling so ill and I was in shock anyway.'

That made perfect sense to Bron. She knew about shock and about pain; and Marged had no one who could have helped her. She had been completely alone in England after her mother had passed away: it had to have been a traumatic time for her. Bron who had been through the pain of the loss of her parents, could appreciate that only too well.

Marged was sitting tensely in her seat, staring ahead. 'I know what you are going through,' Bron said kindly, putting two cappuccinos on the table.

There was a little smile. 'I don't think you do, Bronwen,' she said. 'I don't think you have any idea at all.'

Bron didn't want to argue. 'What I mean is that when I lost my parents. . . .'

'Oh yes, I forgot that. It was a shock for you, their being killed in an accident. But it isn't really the same at all for me.'

'It isn't?'

'No.' There was a long silence, then turning in her seat to look directly at Bron, she said in a cold, rather clipped way, 'My mother was murdered.'

CHAPTER TWO

MURDERED? Bron knew it was a stupid thought but it still came into her head: but murder was something that happened to other people! You read about it in the newspapers, saw it on television. It did not invade her life, or her circle. She had never known anyone that had been murdered . . . until now.

'I don't know what to say. It's too terrible to even think about. Oh, Marged. . . .'

Bron reached out across the Formica table for her cousin's hand. Marged allowed a momentarily squeezing of her hand and then slipped it from Bron's clasp. 'I wish you had let me know. Perhaps there was something I could have done.'

'There was nothing you could have done, Bron. There was no point in my distressing you. Besides, I felt guilty . . .' Marged smiled, a sad little smile. A tear trickled down her cheek and she scraped it away quickly. 'You do feel guilty. You know, if I had not gone out, if she had not been left alone in that big old house. You know how it is – of course, you don't really. You never know unless it happens to you.'

'You don't have to talk about it now if you don't want to. You must be exhausted.'

'Yes I am but I have to stay awake, don't I? And the thought of poor Mum does keep me awake.'

'Do they know who . . . who did it?'

'No. Burglars, a robbery gone wrong – jewellery, they took what there was. I mean someone's life gone for jewellery!'

'This is so terrible, Marged,' Bron murmured. It would not sink in; it seemed so unbelievable. Aunt Lily, murdered, the formidable lady who had always seemed so capable, so in charge of everything, to meet such a terrible end. Her own parents had been killed in a train disaster on the continent. That had seemed bad enough but this – this was an even more horrible way to die.

'I needed to get away, you can see that, and I thought of you, so far away. I thought, I could go to Bron, she and I were always close. You can understand how I needed to get away, can't you, Bron?' Her eyes were large and round and filled with a terrible kind of confusion.

'Of course I understand. I'm so glad you came to me. If I can help in any way you know I will, Marged.' Bron did want to help yet she could not shake off the feeling that there was something rather theatrical in Marged's performance.

'I know you will. You're helping even now, just being able to talk to someone; you have no idea how lonely it was in England.'

Bron could see that. She did not think that Marged and her mother had had any friends; even at school, Marged had seemed different, in a world all of her own, a world that seemed so distant from the twenty-first century. Marged owned no CDs; probably had never been into a dance place or club in her life. Yet she had seemed content. There had been an inner calm about her that Bron, with all

16

her worries and striving, occasionally envied. Of course, there had been the mysterious Denis, the handsome man that Marged had married.

Bron recalled how astounded she had been when Denis had appeared. It seemed so odd; no one ever discovered how they had met, or even how long they had been going out together. The first they knew about it was when they were invited to the registry office wedding. Mischievously, Bron's mother had hinted that perhaps he had made Marged pregnant, but even that proved not to be the case. Then just as he had come into their lives, so he went from it, and there had been no explanation about that. Aunt Lily just said that Denis had left and in such a way that prevented any questions.

'I'll help you get through this,' Bron said, meaning it.

'I'm through it now,' the other girl said somewhat coldly. 'But I need not to be in England because then it all comes back, time and time again. . . .'

'Of course it will do.'

Bron looked at her cousin. Now she seemed in control of herself. It was as if she had little switches inside her that she could click on and off for whatever mood she wished to show. Realizing that was uncharitable, Bron reached across, but before she could clasp her cousin's hand, Marged moved it from the table.

'Let's go now, Bron. I am feeling a little tired.'

'I should think you are more than a little tired. Sorry for keeping you from your bed.'

'Yes, I do need my bed.'

Well, thought Bron, that is me put in my place.

It had just gone dark when they arrived at the house.

'It's lovely here,' Marged said when Bron had switched

on the light.

'I love it, and we have a beautiful garden – we even have grapefruit trees. There's fruit on the trees now – you'll see them in the morning.'

'How amazing – trees with grapefruits on. I've never been abroad, you know.'

'Well, you can't get better than New Zealand, wherever you go.'

'You really like it here, then?'

'I certainly do,' Bron assured her. 'Come and see your room. I'm sure you must be exhausted now.'

'I can wait a moment or two,' Marged said. 'I adore this house! It is so perfect.' She wandered dreamily around the sitting room, touching things, running her hand over the back of the sofa.

Bron could not get the pictures out of her head. The more Marged had talked about what had happened, the more horrible it seemed. She saw in her mind the house in the northern city where Marged had lived all her life. The red-bricked pre-war semi-detached was so solid, so strong. It had a long front garden, and although the house was on a main road, the traffic was not a problem. There were trees in the garden and tall shrubs, a perfect place for a burglar to hide. The front door was not visible from the adjoining house because of the trees. The back of the house was more open because the fence between the properties was only a little over five feet. Then there had been school fields.

There had been no sign of forced entry and although there was a chain on the door, it had not been broken. Whoever it was, Aunt Lily had either let them in or that person had a key.

Aunt Lily had not been a fool; she was not the kind of

person to let a stranger into her house. It would be out of character. Denis's name had come up but no matter how hard the police looked, there was no trace of him. He had completely disappeared. He could have changed his name. He could have emigrated.

For the first time, Bron had found out where Denis had come from. He had lived in the city but he had originally been born and brought up in Yorkshire. There had been a family argument and Denis had left home. He had never been in touch with his family and had not even contacted them when he had married Marged.

'The police contacted his family but they had not seen or heard from him. They were very upset. They said they would have liked to make it up,' Marged had said. 'Anyway, I am sure it hadn't anything to do with Denis. He was such a gentle man. Believe me, there was nothing violent about him at all.'

'I wonder where he went,' Bron now mused, not really wanting to speak out loud. She realized she would have to stop questioning Marged, it was not fair. The girl had come to forget, not be reminded of the tragedy. However, she finished what she had been going to say. 'I have heard of people who have just gone away. They just disappear and it is quite frightening. You would think that people have to be in the records somewhere but they don't.'

'He would have to do something but I think he went abroad.'

'Abroad? But where would he go?' There again, the words slipped out and she wanted to take them back.

'I don't know!' Marged could not hide the irritation. She shrugged impatiently and then yawned. 'I have to sleep,' she declared.

'Of course you do. Forgive me, Marged. I have no right to

ask all these questions. You must be exhausted.'

Bron led her cousin to her bedroom. She had lain out fresh towels and closed the shutters before going to the airport to collect Marged.

'I'm just going to sleep, I'll shower later,' Marged said, opening up her suitcase and rummaging through her stuff until she was able to pull out a filmy nightdress. If Bron had ever thought to buy a gift of nightwear for her cousin, chocolate-coloured fine lace would not have been her first choice. The nightdress was the kind that would be chosen for a honeymoon. There was obviously more to Marged than met the eye, Bron thought, and despite everything, managed a wry smile.

CHAPTER THREE

JACK came that weekend. He was curious about what had happened to Marged's mother, but it was a nasty kind of curiosity. He pretended to be concerned but Bron could see beyond the façade and realized that Jack was getting some kind of vicarious pleasure from the details.

Bron was horrified when he suggested that perhaps Denis had killed the 'old girl' and who could blame him. 'Whatever you do, don't say anything like that to Marged, for goodness' sake!'

'Oh, lighten up, teacher. You are so prim these days!'

Prim? Well, that was a new one, Bron thought. Was I prim when I worked to put you through law school, after you decided to change courses? But she regretted that thought, believing it unworthy of her. She had done it because she loved Jack. Going into teaching had not been something she had wanted to do, but she did it willingly and she had been successful. She had no right to complain, even in her mind, about choices she had made. Jack had not asked her to do it, she had done it willingly.

Marged did not want to go sailing and so Bron went alone. Jack said he would keep her company with rather more eagerness than he had shown for a long time. He would take Marged somewhere for lunch. This altruism was suspicious but Bron was not about to complain. She wanted to get out on the boat again and try to drive the worries out of her.

When Bron arrived back they were already home, playing cards on the deck.

'Did you have a good time?' she asked, since neither of them bothered to ask her how she had enjoyed herself.

'Yes,' Jack answered, 'we went into town. Guess what? We ran into Job Tepi. She's quite smitten with him.'

'I am not!' Marged's face turned puce.

'Well, he is attractive,' Bron said.

'He's a babe magnet,' Jack said, taking on an American accent.

'He's not my type,' Marged said. Now Bron wondered who was being prim.

'He's nice,' Bron said. 'And you will see him again at Ruthie's Burns Night supper.'

'Oh God, I had forgotten that. Must we go?' Jack complained. 'I ask you, celebrating a Scottish poet in this hell hole.'

Hell hole? Bron turned and stared at him, wondering how he could even think of describing the area as that. It was surely one of the most beautiful places on earth. It might not be his cup of tea, enjoying as he did the bright lights, but it was paradise all the same.

'It's not that bad,' Marged said. 'But, Bron, I am going back to Auckland with Jack on Monday. I'm going to stay at his apartment for a couple of days then go down to Christchurch. I want to see a good deal while I am here.'

She was going to stay at Jack's apartment? Bron practically choked on the coke she was drinking. No one got to stay at Jack's apartment. It was very small and even she had been refused a weekend visit.

'It will give her chance to see Auckland,' Jack said, and at least he had the grace to look guilty.

'Well, that's fine, Marged. And good on you for wanting to see more. There's a train that goes to. . . .'

'I'm hiring a car. I want to go to several places. On my way to Wellington I intend to travel over to Napier – I believe it's nice. Then I'll take the ferry. There's quite a lot I want to see.'

'You will be all right driving?' Bron asked.

'Of course. I drove in England; it will be much easier here.'

'That's for sure,' Bron said.

Burns Night Supper was not quite a disaster but Bron found herself embarrassed by Jack. He was clearly drunk even before the meal was served, and he was rude to a couple of people about New Zealand, which was a pretty ungracious way to be, she thought, considering their hosts were New Zealanders.

Job Tepi came alone – last year he had come with a sleek blonde – and looked devastating in a white suit and dark chocolate shirt. She is smitten, Bron thought, when she noticed him talking to Marged. Marged was looking up at him and not saying anything, but her body language said it all.

She did look lovely, Bron thought, in a white floating dress that skimmed her ample curves. She had, for the first time, unwound her hair, and it rippled thick and lustrous over her shoulders. In spite of spending only a little time outside, her skin had turned a very pale golden brown. It was very flattering to her large, golden eyes.

I guess he likes blondes, Bron thought, immediately

shrugging the thought aside; it had nothing to do with her what he liked. Ruthie came over then and gave Bron a huge hug. 'Don't worry,' Job's sister murmured, 'about anything. You're my friend and I love you to bits!'

When did I become sad? Bron questioned herself, because at the words her eyes swam with tears and she had to go to the bathroom. She had always had that touch of Celtic blackness in her soul – from her mother, she guessed – but now she was feeling really melancholy and it was not like her. Her life was imploding and there was nothing she could do to stop it.

Straightening her shoulders, she went back into the party. In the narrow passage, she met Job. 'You OK?' he asked, resting a hand on her shoulder. 'You looked upset.'

'I did? Oh, these kinds of events make me come over all emotional.'

'Homesick?'

'No, I love it here.'

'Good. I like your sash, it suits you.'

She fingered the tartan sash she had bought. It was a MacDonald clan tartan, which she thought was neutral.

'Jack says I have no right to wear it, being Welsh and not Scottish.'

He laughed. 'Well, look at me.' He flashed his cufflinks which bore the cross of St Andrew. 'So how Scots do I look to you?'

'Not very.' She smiled up at him. 'Thanks, Job. I'm having a great time!'

Jack did not come home the following weekend. He did not telephone either. She rang but there was no answer. He couldn't have gone somewhere with Marged because he said she had left. Anyway, if she hadn't gone or was still there, Bron was not going to throw a hissy if he took her out and about.

Her getting in touch with Jack started to become very important. After all, she had gone to Ninety Mile Beach with Job Tepi and she needed to tell him before someone else did. Not that there was anything in it. Job had called round and said he had to go up there. She had once said she would love to see it and he had remembered.

It had been nothing special; they had driven up there in his off-road vehicle, and then driven along the glorious beach.

It had been exhilarating and exciting. There she was, speeding through ripples of the Pacific Ocean. It was a long way from the northern town she had been brought up in. There had been nothing to feel guilty about but somehow she felt she had gone behind Jack's back. But didn't he do that? He had cut her from his life, not vice versa.

These days he usually contacted her through e-mails rather than phone calls, which gave him an escape clause. He could tell her anything and she would not know it was a lie. But what would he have to lie to her about? She had to get control of herself, yet she could not get over the suspicion that something was wrong. Perhaps he had met someone else. If he had, why not be up front and tell her? Why play around like this? Their marriage hadn't been great for a long time, she admitted to herself. She looked at what had been missing. Friendship was gone, there was not that camaraderie they had had as students. Yet hadn't that gone in England? Perhaps she had not noticed because she had always been working so hard. Sex? Running a hand through her sleek, bobbed hair, she told herself she was not going to go there, no way!

When days went by, she grew increasingly angry. He

25

could have told her *something*. Just what was he playing at?

She rang the flat on two more evenings and sent e-mails. In the end she decided she had to ring the office. Jack had told her not to ring the office during the week; he was frequently busy with clients and the partners were not keen on private telephone calls. Every call had to be logged and the girl who took calls was fussy about keeping a perfect record. She was a nasty, shifty-eyed little bitch, he had said.

However, the voice on the telephone was friendly and warm and not at all like the pernickety girl that Jack had described.

'I'm sorry to trouble you, but could I speak to Mr Mellor? It's his wife speaking.'

'Mr Mellor?' the girl said, a faint question in her voice. 'Could you hold a second?'

The second stretched to minutes; checking her watch, she saw four minutes had slipped by. If Jack were with a client he would be angry that she had disturbed him.

'Mrs Mellor?' It was a male voice, well spoken with a slight New Zealand accent.

'Speaking. I . . . I wanted to speak to my husband. I know it's probably silly but I've been ringing the flat and I can't seem to get hold of him.'

'You can't speak to him here, I'm afraid,' he said. 'Mrs Mellor, I don't really know how to say this but Jack doesn't work for us any more. He hasn't worked for us since November. Mrs Mellor, are you there. . . ?'

She felt dizzy; a cold yet clammy perspiration broke out over her body. Her heart felt as if it had stopped, then it started racing. She gripped the wall, her palm so damp her hand slid against the plaster, leaving a wet imprint.

'I'm sorry? I don't understand.'

'Mrs Mellor.' The man sounded so kind, so reasonable, even though he had to be playing some kind of practical joke on her. 'Look, why don't you come into the city? Perhaps you need to talk to me.'

'No, I need to talk to Jack . . . is he there?'

'Mrs Mellor, I can't do this on the phone. I can only say that Jack is no longer with us.'

'But he went to work a week last Monday, to Auckland. He left with my cousin. He e-mailed me to say he was working at the weekend.'

'Mrs Mellor, Jack never worked at the weekend. It's company policy that our staff don't.'

She demanded. 'Who is this?'

'It's Barry Clarkson, Mrs Mellor.'

Barry Clarkson: tall, well built, about fifty, greying hair, the senior partner. She had met him once; he had seemed a charming, sensible man.

'If I come there tomorrow. . . .'

'You do that, Mrs Mellor. Come any time. I can make myself free.'

'Thank you.' She put the phone down, then turned and rested her back against the wall. Eventually she slid down until she was sitting on the floor. She was shaking. It was hot in the house yet she felt chilled, as if she had the flu or something.

Sensibly, she recognized the symptom of shock, yet it took a while for her to pull herself up and to stagger into the kitchen to put on the kettle. She made herself a cup of tea and forced herself to sit at the kitchen table as she sipped it. Slowly the shaking eased; it left her feeling weak, as if she had had a bad fall.

For a long time she sat mulling over the facts. All these

weeks Jack had been deceiving her, letting her believe he had been working at the firm of lawyers. He was using work as an excuse for not coming home. He did not fear her, so that was not behind his deception. He certainly was not so afraid of her he could not tell her he had left the company, far from it.

Perhaps he had gone to another firm and had not wanted her to know in case she worried. She knew he was not really happy in New Zealand but he was trying to adjust. That was it; he had found another firm to take him on and wanted to see how it worked out before he told her about it. No sense in worrying her more than necessary.

He had to be working: he ran his car, rented the flat. Unless . . . She stood and waited a moment to see if the dizziness came back but she was all right. She went into the small study and into the drawer where they kept the bank statements. Taking out the ringbinder they were kept in, she opened it and saw it was empty. There were no bank statements. Feeling tension building, she went through all the drawers, looking and searching. There was a chequebook to their joint account. They seldom wrote cheques, just for utility bills. It was a new chequebook. The old chequebook was not there, nor was the chequebook stubs that she had a habit of keeping for a month or two. There was nothing.

The rest of the drawers were empty. It was as if someone had cleaned everything out, and it wasn't her because she was not that methodical. Neither was Jack! He left everything to do with money to her. They did not have a mortgage. The house they sold in England, as well as part of the legacy her parents had left to her, more than enabled them to buy their house outright. There were only the utility bills to pay. Her own salary went into the bank as did

Jack's. Although they had, like any married couple, issues, money had never been one of them.

The day lay before her; she knew it would drag endlessly towards night. She could not concentrate on anything and so decided that she would drive to Auckland there and then. She packed a couple of items in a bag and then locked up the house after calling Ruthie to tell her she would be away.

Ruthie wanted to chat and Bron let her get on with it. If she acted as she really felt she knew it would arouse suspicion and she did not want to tell anyone that she was worried about Jack, or what she had discovered about Jack's job.

'Ruthie, I have to go now. It's a long drive and I want to get there before dark,' Bron said, but in a friendly, teasing tone that fooled the other woman.

'OK, OK, I know I love to gossip. I'll see you when you get back – come over, we can have dinner or lunch, whatever.'

'Lovely, I'll do that.'

Before setting off, Bron opened all the windows of her car; she did not have the benefit of air conditioning and knew it would be a hot drive on such a day. When she reached Whangarei she was held up some time by roadworks.

The sun was setting by the time she reached Auckland. Jack's flat was in the city just off Queen Street and she managed to reach it before it went dark. There was parking for residents beneath the building, but she didn't have a pass so she found a parking place on the street, and walked back to the building. The flat was on the third floor. When she reached the door she pressed her ear against the wood just in case there was any sound. Silence came back to her.

Sliding the key in the door, she turned it, and then, as if she didn't have a right to be there, she stepped quickly inside.

There was a small hallway, which was very dark, and her fingers felt along the wall for a light switch. It took some time for her to feel the location and then when she put down the switch, nothing happened.

She felt her way along the wall in pitch black. Even taking what she imagined were big strides, it seemed a long time before the hard roundness of a door handle pressed against her hand. Eagerly, she turned it, pushing the door.

It was very dim but a slender beam of light from a street-light filtered through the window. She felt for the switch and again nothing happened. At first she thought it was the darkness that was hiding things but on looking more closely it appeared the room was empty.

Bron crossed the wooden floorboards, squeezing her eyelids as if this would give her the ability to see more clearly. She was in the small living room, and it was empty of furniture. She pushed the door on the right-hand side of the wall and this let into the small bedroom. It was pitch black in there because there was no window. Re-crossing the small lounge, she went into the kitchen; the same meagre light sneaked in through the windows. The kitchen, fitted with wooden units, was devoid of kitchen utensils or any sign of food. *She could not stay here.*

Hurriedly she crossed the lounge and felt her way along the hall, thankful that she had not locked the outer door. She slid through it, closing it softly behind her as if she was a thief, and then she locked the door.

It occurred to her to ask neighbours if they knew anything, yet she was exhausted and not a little frightened. She needed to sort out her mind before investigating anything. Close by she knew there was a hotel and only hoped that they had a room. Desperately she needed to lie down, to think, to worry. . . .

She sat on the bed waiting for the tea she had ordered to arrive. Her body was trembling; she pulled at the duvet and wrapped it around herself. She had turned off the cooler but it was shock that had its grip on her and not temperature.

The tea helped when it came. After sipping from the cup, she pulled off her clothes and scrambled into the bed, tucking herself up in the duvet before reaching for the cup once more.

Where was Jack? What was he up to? He had to have his laptop because the e-mails had not come back. He had to know she was worried yet he could not even have the courtesy to get in touch with her. Damn him! She felt like going back home and not bothering. Yet some sense of right impelled her to see it through. She had to get to the bottom of it, all of it.

After she had telephoned Mr Clarkson, on waking from a fitful night's sleep, they agreed that she should go to his office at 10.30. It gave her time to pull herself together. She felt lousy, as if she had a hangover, although she had not had anything alcoholic to drink. Trying to fend off this feeling, she took a long cold shower and felt only marginally better afterwards.

It would take her twenty minutes to get to the office. She thought she knew the way but stopped at the reception desk to make sure. There was a bus that stopped close by the building, she was told, but a brisk walk, in her present mood, seemed preferable.

The city was busy; there seemed to be a lot of tourists as well as people going about their business.

In her present state of mind she found the city oddly threatening but knew it was ridiculous. Auckland was a safe city compared with some, but life in the slow lane in the far north had made her a little panicky where crowds were concerned. Once or twice she was jostled by accident, and it made her walk closer to the buildings. It was a horrible feeling and one she had never experienced before. You're a city girl, she told herself, trying to chivvy herself along, but her efforts were in vain. She felt battered and frightened and very much alone.

The girl at reception was pretty; sitting waiting for Mr Clarkson to come and take her to his office, she was aware that she was looking at her slyly. Bron had chosen to wear the one dress she had brought with her, a sleeveless cotton fitted dress in a flattering shade of deep pink. She thought the colour gave the message that she was confident and assured, but judging by the looks that the receptionist was casting in her direction, she guessed that her choice of dress was wrong and that it did nothing of the sort.

'Mrs Mellor.' She stood when the man called her name. She recognized him immediately. Tall and built more like a rugby forward than she had remembered, he was also much younger than her memory had recalled. When she had met him at a firm's function, she had taken to him right away. He seemed kind and friendly. 'Do come through.'

His office was comfortable and neat. There was not the usual pile of files that, in her experience, lawyers had in their offices. He indicated a comfortable chair at the side of his desk; there were two chairs and he took the other instead of going to sit behind his desk. To his question as to whether she would like coffee, she said, yes she would.

'I am so sorry, Mrs Mellor, all this must be a terrible shock to you.'

'It is. I don't understand. I went to the flat. It's . . . it's empty, totally empty.' Bron met his sympathetic gaze and then looked away, running a hand nervously over her dark brown hair. 'I feel something has gone terribly wrong, that something terrible has happened to Jack.'

He said nothing. She liked the fact that he did not try to reassure her that Jack would be all right; he could not know that any more than she could. The girl came in with coffee. Bron said black would be fine. The slightly bitter taste jolted her out of her lethargy.

'What happened, Mr Clarkson? Please be frank. I really need that.'

'I wouldn't be any other. Bronwen, isn't it?'

'Yes,' she acknowledged, not bothering to give him the diminutive.

'We had to let Jack go.'

She noted the euphemism. 'You sacked him?'

'Yes.' He did not bother to prevaricate.

'Can I ask why? Was it his work?'

'Nothing was the matter with his work. There were certain irregularities. I am so sorry to have to do this, Bronwen.'

'Don't worry about it. I have to know . . . have to get to the bottom of it.'

'A client's account, money being appropriated, it was that kind of thing.'

Money appropriated. She wished the lawyer would be more frank. He was obviously hinting that Jack was stealing money from a client. *Jack?* It seemed so unlikely.

'Jack? I can't see it. Jack isn't short of money; neither of us are. Oh, we don't live life in the fast lane or have millions stashed away, but compared to some we are comfortable.'

'I'm sure it must sound ridiculous to you. It did to us, for a while, and then we had absolute proof. I confronted Jack and he admitted it. He said he was in debt and needed the extra cash to pay someone off.'

'I can't believe this!' she said, clasping a hand around her throat. 'It just doesn't seem like Jack. I mean, we had no debts. He doesn't gamble or anything. I can't understand it, Mr Clarkson. I just can't!'

'I don't know why he was in debt, only that he told me he was. Now and again a man came to see him. He wasn't a client and sometimes I've seen them in town together. In fact, before we discovered the discrepancy in his client's account, I saw Jack and this man in the street. They were arguing and it seemed rather fierce.'

'It just does not sound like Jack,' she protested yet again, wondering who this man was who was pretending to be Jack. Then she realized it had to be Jack. She could not use that for an excuse. Jack was a Janus and she had better realize that. Barry Clarkson was no fool. She had to admit that there were things about her husband that she did not understand, or know about. 'Who was this man you saw with Jack? Do you know?'

'Jack never introduced us. He was a tall, well-built man, a Maori, I think. Longish dark hair, very well and very expensively dressed.'

The only person she knew who fitted that description was Job Tepi yet it was incredible that he would be arguing with Jack, or visiting him at his office. She only saw him up north, usually when he was in casual gear, but she knew

34

when he did dress up he looked like a million dollars.

'Was he young?'

'Mid thirties, I would guess. A very good-looking man.'

Bron nodded, keeping to herself the knowledge that she thought she knew who it was. Surely it could only be Job Tepi.

If Job was involved with Jack then why had she never been aware of it? If he was the person demanding money from Jack, what could it be for? Drugs? She was letting her imagination get the better of her. Jack was definitely not involved with drugs and she doubted that Job Tepi was either. But how did she know *anything*?

Job was wealthy, everyone said so. He had the hotels, or maybe more than the two she knew about. She did not know where he made his money but he was not flash and did not throw money around. He lived in a beautiful house, Ruthie had told her, and he had his boat, but he did not drive a very expensive car. Surely it could not be Job Tepi? He was *so* normal! She could have smiled in ordinary circumstances; after all she had thought Jack *so* normal and look what she was now discovering about her husband.

Before showing her out of his office, Barry Clarkson said, 'Perhaps it all got too much for Jack and he decided to go away. I know he was not happy over here. Perhaps he's gone home.'

'But without telling me? Mr Clarkson, we were more than just a married couple, we were friends. We've known each other since we were students. If Jack was in trouble he could have come to me. He knew he could always count on me.'

The older man pressed a hand on her shoulder. 'He obviously forgot that, Bronwen, otherwise you would not be having this conversation with me.'

She had tried to save face in the office but once outside she stood for a while taking deep breaths; her mind was reeling and she felt sick with worry. Jack had somehow got himself in a terrible mess and for some crazy reason had not thought to come to her with his problems. But what could she do? Go to the police?

Jack had not been working, of that Barry Clarkson was certain, since he would have had to give a reference and no requests for a reference had been received. Besides, the law firms were a closely knit community, and other firms would surely sense that something was wrong because Jack had been sacked so abruptly. He was lucky Mr Clarkson had taken pity on him and not called in the police. The lawyer had managed to straighten out the missing money without the client being aware of the original misappropriation. They had been so good to Jack when they had had every right to ruin him.

She trudged, in the rather sweaty heat, back downtown. She would go to the flat again and in daylight give the place a thorough search. There had to be a clue to where he had gone. He had to have been at the flat last week because he had taken Marged there. *Marged.* She had not given a thought to her – perhaps Jack had gone to Christchurch with her. Yet Marged had left when Bron had last spoken to Jack, and anyway why, being in such a mess, would be go off to Christchurch with her? The idea was ludicrous.

The key slid into the lock but when she came to turn it, the lock refused to move. She took out the key and examined it to make sure it was the same key that she had used the previous night. She tried it again; it would not click open. Someone had changed the lock. That was the only explanation. She rapped on the door with her knuckles.

The door swung open, just as she was about to turn away.

A man stood on the threshold, a small wiry man, an Asian man, probably from Indonesia. 'Yes?' he asked, his eyes narrowing. She knew she must have looked distressed. After the morning she had had, she could not look any other way.

'I came here last night. I'm looking for the man that lived here. This is his flat.'

'I knew that!' the man snapped back at her. His English was good. He had only the slightest of accents.

'You did?'

'Of course! Why do you think I changed the lock? That bloke left – he owes me rent. Do you know him?'

'You're the owner?'

'You must be joking. I work for the managing company. They are not happy he left. Who are you?'

'When did he go?' she asked, delaying telling him anything until she could find something in return.

'How do I know? I came round yesterday to collect and he'd gone. The neighbours said they haven't seen him for five days. I guess I should have come sooner.'

Bron looked at him, wondering whether to just leave after telling a lie, but she could not do it. Some sense of decency prevented her from just walking away.

'I'm his wife. I don't know where he's gone.'

'Yeah, I believe you,' he sneered. 'We'll be paying you a visit, you can count on that.'

'How much rent does he owe?' she asked, not bothering to say again that she did not know where Jack had gone. He obviously would not believe her.

'A month's.'

'I can pay that,' she offered.

'OK, but no cheques. We have had enough of his bouncing beauties!'

He obviously meant cheques but how could Jack be writing cheques that bounced? They had the one bank account between them.

'I'll get the cash,' she said. 'Tell me where your office is and I'll take it there.'

The man laughed without humour. 'You think I'd fall for that? I'll come with you.'

'Look, I'm not going to give you all that cash. How do I know you'll pay it in?'

'Because it's more than my life's worth not to hand it in. These are serious people. They don't like bad debtors or having thieves working for them.'

'I'm sorry but I still want to pay the money into the office.'

'OK, have it your own way. They won't be pleased to see you but I suppose you can take the abuse.'

'I don't think they are likely to abuse me if I am paying them money.'

'You'd be surprised. And when you *find* your husband, tell him we don't forget.'

There was a cash machine at a bank a couple of streets from the apartment. Bron drew out the sum of money, carefully folding the dollars and slipping them into an inside pocket of her handbag. The office was on Karanghape Road; Jack used to laugh about K Road, as he called it, and said it was notorious at night, but it seemed all right to Bron. Everywhere looked better, she supposed, in daylight. With the exception of the Champs-Elysées, she thought ridiculously, which looked gorgeous at night.

They had gone to Paris for their honeymoon – corny but wonderful. The memories flooded her mind. Paris in the autumn. They had sat at pavement cafés and made their glasses of cheap red wine last for hours, just people-watching and holding hands. Tears threatened to erupt; she shook her head as if this would disperse the images that were flooding into her mind.

A surly girl who wore far too much make-up was behind a desk. The office left much to be desired, and a quick look around did not inspire Bron with confidence. A man came out eventually. He was huge, tall and bulky, obviously from one of the islands – the Solomon Islands, she guessed.

'So, you want to pay Jack's rent. Just where's he gone, by the way?'

'I wish I knew,' Bron said, meeting his malevolent gaze and determined not to be made afraid or to be intimidated.

'You're lucky then,' he said. 'Give me the money.' He stretched out a large hand. It was dimpled like a baby's bottom.

'You can give me a receipt and I will need to sign something that ends the lease.'

'Well, you're no fool,' he laughed. 'OK, Doreen, get the old lease out for flat fifteen, Mellor's place, and get me a receipt.'

Doreen, surprising Bron, moved quietly and efficiently, and she brought the receipt and the lease to the desk in moments. The man looked at the lease. 'I could make you pay till the end of the lease,' he said.

'Well, if you want to do that, I'll have my solicitor, Mr Barry Clarkson, contact you. I think we need to—'

'No need for that. I said I *could*, didn't say I *would*. Doreen, make a photocopy of this lease.'

When the photocopy was done, he put a red line through it and wrote 'Lease cancelled'.

'We've got someone for the flat, anyway. Someone's been wanting it for a while.'

'Good,' Bron said coldly. Then she took out the money, the crisp dollar bills seeming to disappear in the man's huge fist.

'Cash, I like cash,' he said.

'Who owns the building?' she asked suddenly as the thought occurred to her.

'Why do you want to know that? Got a complaint for them?'

'Not at all, I am just curious. You obviously manage the building for someone.'

'Sure. Do I look like I own a block of apartments in Auckland?' He laughed. 'Tepi owns it; he lives up your way. Job Tepi . . . know him?'

'Not really,' she lied tightly.

'Well, Jack did. OK, Missus, I suppose that's it. Nice to have known you.'

It was very late when Bron arrived home. She wondered how she had managed to drive so far in the state she was in. The blessing was that she had set off late and there had not been much traffic after she left Auckland.

The house retained the heat of two days but it felt good as it wrapped itself around her. She went to bed straight away, pulling off her clothes and scattering them as she went to the bedroom. The bed felt blissful, she wrapped the cotton sheet around her and closed her eyes and listened to the silence. Her last thoughts were that she would never fall asleep. The next thing she knew, it was daylight. Somehow she had twisted her body around the sheet and it took a while for her to untangle herself.

Practically half asleep, she went to the shower, turning it full on and standing beneath the cool battering jets of water without moving.

'This is a nightmare, this is a nightmare,' she said over and over again, and then she reached for the shower gel and poured it over herself, soaping herself thoroughly as if this would cleanse her of all her fears and worries, as if it would miraculously allow her to be fully awake in a world that was unchanged.

The bread was stale but not green, so she shoved a slice in the toaster. The coffee was soon made, and she spread butter liberally on the toast. It tasted all right. The silence was all around her; she turned on the radio then found the noise jarring and switched it off.

The events of the previous day started to seep into her mind. The pain, the humiliation, these emotions would not let her rest.

What had she discovered? That her husband was a thief, there was no polite way to say it. He had lied and cheated and he had gone, God alone knew where, to escape the net that was tightening around him.

If only . . . if only . . . the two words beat away inside her. *If only he had told her.* What would she have done? She was imagining that she would be reasonable and understanding but she would not have been. She would have been wild with anger and resentment. She was no saint and she had better stop painting herself as such.

When she had gone to pay the hotel bill, her credit card had been refused. She had stood there, other people at the desk, her face crimson with embarrassment. Things like that did not happen to her. Again she had visited the cash withdrawal facility, and with forethought pressed the key for a statement.

She had, with what she had taken out to pay the management company and her hotel bill, just $300 in the bank. What had happened to her salary? She had had far

41

more money in the bank than she had paid out during the day. There was over two months' salary in there. Of course, he had taken it; she telephoned the bank before setting off for home. Even their savings account had been closed. She had nothing but those $300.

Real anger took hold of her, it took hold of her confusion and smashed it to pieces. Real anger was good, though, and that much she appreciated, because it somehow got the adrenaline racing.

Before leaving Auckland she went to the police station. A thirty-year-old man missing, having taken money, was not really police business. The money was half his, anyway; their account was a joint account. They could list him as a missing person, but really if he wanted to disappear from his marriage, well, that was up to him.

'But suppose something really serious has happened to him?' she implored.

'Like what? Do you think he was likely to be killed or something?' the young officer asked.

'Well no, but . . . anything could have happened.'

'If something has happened, then that will turn up. Don't worry, probably a mid-life crisis.'

A *mid-life crisis!* She wanted to scream, but then thought better of it. It was not the policeman's fault, and he was right. Jack had planned his escape very well. It was hardly likely that, if something had happened to him, the money would have been taken from her bank account, or that her credit card would have been refused.

After she left the police station, she knew what she would do: she would seek out Jack herself, no matter the cost. She would not let him just disappear.

The first thing she would do would be to sell the boat. That would raise some cash. There were four weeks before she was due back at school. That should give her time. She was not worried about Jack now, she realized, as she washed her breakfast dishes. She was angry, furious and in an unforgiving mood. He had betrayed her in the cruellest of ways; all she wanted now was an end to it. After that she could start to rebuild her own life.

Since Marged had been staying with them, Bron had only been down to the boat once. She loved to be on the water and knew it was the one thing she would miss. Perhaps when she got down there she would take the boat out for one last cruise around and then see the marina manager about putting her up for sale.

Job Tepi's vehicle was in the car park. He was the one person she did not want to see. Somehow he had a relationship with Jack that she knew nothing about. He was Jack's landlord and had never said anything. His duplicity was doubly wounding because she had really liked Job and thought him honest as well as reliable. The people he had managing his property were hardly awe-inspiring types. She thought of the seedy office and the two men she had met. No, he was not the trustworthy and reliable type she had at first imagined.

Down at the very bottom of her she had expected it; she had not wanted to acknowledge it but it had been there niggling away at her. She ought not to have been surprised, not to feel the anger swelling inside her once more, or the bitter taste of real hate on her tongue. The boat was not at its mooring. Job was there, on his boat. He saw her on the pontoon and called out. She whirled away, going in the direction of the manager's office.

He was inside and gave her a friendly greeting. 'The boat's been sold?' she asked.

He looked amazed, pushing his baseball cap to the back of his head.

'Why, yes, didn't you know Jack had sold it?' he asked, scratching the thin patch of hair that he had revealed.

'No, I didn't. Who did he sell it to?' she asked, taking a deep breath, half expecting him to say Job Tepi.

'Some bloke from Auckland. He came down last week, sailed the boat back up. Mrs Mellor, are you OK? You look terrible.'

'I'm fine.' The waves of anger were accelerating her heartbeat, so much so she thought she would collapse. She felt as if she were hungry and dizzy and she stepped back, colliding with someone. Turning, she saw it was Job Tepi. He reached out an arm to steady her.

'Don't bother!' she spat, shrugging out of his touch. Then she walked out, careful not to slam the door behind her. She ran, then, back to the car park, the heat of the sun searing her back. When she reached the car she collapsed on the front seat, resting her head against the steering wheel, waiting for it all to go away. She knew with a terrible kind of logic that this was not the end of it.

'Bron, listen to me. . . .' Job Tepi was there, his head in the open window. She went to turn the key to start the engine but he was quicker than her and he grabbed hold of the keys.

'Don't be despicable! Give me the keys. I don't want to talk to you.'

'Yes, you do. And if you won't talk you certainly will listen.'

'If you don't leave me alone, I'll call the police.'

'Do it,' he said. She reached in her handbag for her mobile phone, stuff spilling out over the seat. Before she could retrieve the phone and dial the numbers, Job was in the car. She tried to open the driver's door but he had locked it.

'I know that Jack's done a bunk,' he said flatly.

'I expect you do. I even guess that you know where he is.'

'Of course I don't,' Job said. 'If I did do you think I'd be sitting here.'

'I paid his rent.'

'I know and more fool you. Do you think I'd let *them* come after *you*? He won't get very far,' Job said, and there was a chilling threat in his voice. 'But you need to sort things out, Bron, and sort them out right now.'

'Like what?'

'Like getting the house protected, that's what.'

'What do you mean?' she asked, fear creeping coldly along her spine.

'Before he cuts you out of that too. Look, he's sold the bloody boat. Don't you think he's thought about raising cash on the house.'

'He can't do that without my signature.'

Job laughed without humour. 'Do you know your husband at all?'

'Not as well as you,' she spat, 'obviously!'

'I can't deny that. I guess I'm a better judge of people than you are. So are you going to protect the house or not?'

She waited a long time, considering what he had said. She wondered if she could tell him to go to hell but unfortunately she had too much common sense for that. He was right in what he said. After everything that Jack had done to her, how could she expect him to leave the house, bought and paid for outright, to sit there, all that money wrapped up in it?

'Do I need a lawyer?' she asked.

'Sure you do. Give me your mobile.' She passed it to him

and he keyed in some numbers.

'I need to see Matthews today. No, that won't do . . . I said today . . . I'm leaving right now . . . OK, will be there.'

She heard a different kind of man; she had never known that he could be so authoritative or downright rude.

'Where are your deeds?' he asked after he ended the call.

'At the bank.'

'Thank God for that. OK, let's go get them. . . .'

'But what can I do? I can't put the house solely in my name.'

'Sure you can. He would have done.'

'But that's not legal.'

He shrugged. 'There's ways and means. If you're fighting a crook you don't use legal means.'

'I can't do this,' she protested.

'Then risk losing everything, Bron, it's your choice!'

'How do I know I can trust you, or your lawyer?'

'You don't, but what else are you going to do?'

She let him take her to the bank; that could not do her any harm. Anyway, in her heart she suspected it was too late. Jack would have removed the deeds already. She thought Job Tepi thought that too, so when the bank manager produced the deeds, she could not be sure who was the more surprised.

The bank manager said, 'I know you wanted to raise money on the house. Mr Mellor spoke to me about it but I told him to bring you along and we could discuss it. Do you still want to do that?'

'I owe you a huge thank you,' Bron said. 'You don't know how appreciative I am for your doing that.'

'Well, that's how it's done with joint ownership. Didn't he want you to know?' he asked, curiosity fighting a losing battle with professionalism.

'No, he didn't.'

The older man pursed his lips; he felt a little burst of pride that he had played by the rules. He had never altogether liked Jack Mellor but he said nothing to the wife. He glanced at Job Tepi and wondered what he had to do with it all, but this time did not give way to curiosity.

'We have to go,' Job said, 'if we want to get to Whangarei on time.'

'Are you taking the deeds?' the bank manager asked.

'For now.' It was Tepi who answered.

'I would keep them safe,' he persisted.

'I know that and you have done but Jack and I are coming to an arrangement. We need to meet with a lawyer.' She smiled and he responded. Mrs Mellor he did like. There was an elfin beauty about her that he found particularly attractive. In his eyes she was Audrey Hepburn but with more flesh.

They did not speak as Job drove them; it was comfortable in the car since it had air conditioning. Bron was nursing resentment and anger and at the same time wondering why she was trusting Job Tepi, who knew a lot more than he had ever revealed. Yet there was no alternative. She had never done anything illegal in her life. She knew she had to prevent Jack getting his hands on the deeds of the house, otherwise she would be left to pay off any debts and have no home. She felt physically sick, and it was not the twisting roads that caused the nausea. She put her hands on to the dashboard, bending her head a little.

'Are you all right?' Job asked.

'No, of course I'm not all right.' She heard the waspish quality in her voice but she could not seem to help it.

'Do you want to stop?' he asked.

'No . . . I'm not sick, at least not physically, it's just that reality is setting in. I'm just furious and I don't trust *you* either.'

'Thank you for that,' he bit back.

'Well, what do you expect? You knew what Jack was up to. You knew he was spending too much money and he could not pay his rent. You never told me,' she accused. 'You never even let on to me that you owned the building where he had his flat. How much else have you been keeping from me?'

'Whoa, hold on there, it was not my place to dob him in.'

'I thought you were *my* friend. Obviously I was wrong about that too.'

He said nothing. She gave him a quick look, saw that he had paled ever so slightly and that his hands were gripping the steering wheel way too tightly.

'Just what was he doing? How could he spend all that money?'

'At first he was playing cards. . . .'

'Playing cards?' she said aghast. 'Jack never played cards.'

'I don't know about that. I believe he joined in with some high flyers, got in debt to them and had to pay them or else. I suppose it all got a bit too much and he decided to do a runner.'

'I should never have left him with time on his hands in Auckland.'

'Listen, Bronwen, don't blame yourself.' She noticed he used her full name. Obviously he was still angry with her. 'He had a great time in the city. He didn't go short of anything, and I mean anything.'

'Just what do you mean by that?' she asked, her voice sharp with anger.

'Think about it!'

'Do you mean women?' she asked. 'I don't believe that.'

'Please yourself,' he said coldly.

Why was she being like this? Defending Jack when what he had done was indefensible? When she knew as well that it all had to be true. Jack had not made love to her in ages; he avoided going to bed with her, staying up later than her and being up and about early in the morning, or feigning sleep when she had occasionally wrapped her arms around him. It came to her, flashing through her mind and causing her to close her eyes. The truth was she had not been bothered anyway about that side of their marriage. Not for a very long time.

'I don't think the earth ever moved,' she murmured to herself, and when she felt Job glance at her briefly, realized she had spoken out loud.

'What?' he asked brusquely.

'Just muttering to myself,' she said, blushing.

He let it go and she dipped once more into her private thoughts. Yet they had had something precious, surely? Sex was not the be-all and end-all of everything; they had been friends. There were so many shared good times, or had she been fooling herself all the while? Concentrating solely on their time at uni. Sure they had been happy then? They were young and having a good time. They had no money but lots of ambition. It had been the best time of their lives.

Later in their marriage, when she had lost her parents so shockingly, her whole life had revolved around making Jack happy; perhaps she had been a limpet and he had grown tired of it. Bitterness flowed through her. He had used her, taking ruthless advantage of her generosity and vulnerability. He had known she was alone in the world. Apart from cousin Marged, there was no one else. How convenient that had been for him.

I don't want to be this way, she said to herself, this time keeping the words deep inside. I don't want to be a bitter and twisted person. Jack has done a terrible thing but maybe some good will come out of it. Perhaps I'll learn to stand on my own two feet and not need anyone in my life. I have a great career; I don't need anything else. That it was not the career she had envisaged for herself did not matter just then.

'We're here.' Job Tepi disturbed her thoughts. 'Do you trust me enough to let me do the talking?'

'You'd better,' she said, 'because I don't even understand why I am here.'

'You're here to save your home,' he said.

She was glad she let him do it all; she would not have known what to say to the lawyer apart from, 'I don't want Jack to get hold of the house'. The lawyer explained everything to her and it was straightforward enough. She felt safe and it was all quite legal, which was a relief.

'He can come for a share but he can't get hold of more than that,' the lawyer explained. 'And if he comes for a share he might not be able to get all of it, because of the way he has cleaned you out.'

In the end she signed an affidavit concerning all that had happened and Job witnessed it. Job also produced evidence of Bron paying the outstanding rent.

'Did you sign your half of the boat over to him?' Job asked.

'No,' Bron said.

'I know the guy who bought it. The documents he got were made out in Jack's name only. He must have changed the documentation, somehow forged your signature.'

Bron looked at both men helplessly; she could see that

the lawyer felt pity for her and hated it. She had been a fool but she was not stupid, yet who would believe that of her? All she had been doing was trusting the man she had married.

'It could be difficult to prove unless the signature is a poor one. You need to get a copy of this document then you can see. If you ever find it, which I doubt you will. Then if it looks dodgy we can do something.'

'I can have a word with the man that bought the boat,' Job said. 'Like I said, I know him quite well. But really I don't think he'll be able to help. Jack probably destroyed the original documents. If he had any sense that's what he would have done.'

He knew way too much, Bron thought, feeling anger rise against him once more. Yet he was trying to help her now. Maybe he regretted his various dealings with Jack, but she did not like it that he had kept quiet. She could not say anything about it yet, at least not in the lawyer's office.

'Let's get something to eat,' he suggested, 'before we go back.'

They found a Chinese restaurant and went inside. Bron was not even hungry yet she knew she had eaten nothing but the stale piece of bread all day. She would order something light, if there was such a thing, and told Job so.

'Have an omelette,' he suggested. 'They make good omelettes here. I know it's not Chinese food but it will be good for you if you feel rough.'

'I do feel rough,' she admitted. 'I feel as if I've been kicked by stampeding stallions.' She tried to smile. 'You know, I just want to get on with my life now.'

'Look . . .' He leaned over and touched her hand with his, she moved her hand away. He moved his arm from the table. 'If you want to know where Jack is I might be able to help.'

'I don't give a damn where he is!' she snapped. 'I really don't,' she emphasized, yet her eyes felt hot with unshed tears. 'Excuse me.' She left the table, going into the ladies room.

It was so ridiculous; she was not crying for Jack, she was crying for herself, for her foolishness, for not seeing that everything around her was disintegrating. Her tears were brief; she made herself stop, splashed cold water on her face and straightened her shoulders before going out to join Job. She was strong, she was not going to cave in over this. She would start over, she had to do that.

He had ordered her a glass of cool white wine, although for himself he took sparkling water. 'Cheers,' he said, in a mock British accent. She nodded and then sipped the wine. Their food came and they ate in silence. It was fairly companionable and he had been right – the omelette was really delicious and just what she needed.

When they had finished and were having coffee, he said, 'Here's to new beginnings for you, Bron,' raising his cup.

'Thank you,' she said. 'I hope I can make the best of them.'

'You will. You're that kind of person.'

'You don't know anything about me.' She could not stop the bitterness.

'I think I know more than you think. Look, just because Jack pulled the wool over your eyes, it doesn't mean you are a simpleton. You trusted someone, they let you down. It happens all the time. Some people are just so clever at conning people.'

'You'd know about that I suppose.'

'What do you mean, Bron?'

'You hang about with some shady characters,' she said.

'I do?'

'Those guys in Auckland . . . at the rental office.'

He had the nerve to smile. 'Appearances can be decep-
tive, Bron, as you should know by now. Anyway, if you want
someone collecting rent you don't want the Pope.'

She looked up at him, wanting to say something smart
but nothing came into her head. Besides, he was probably
right.

'I guess not,' she admitted.

'I'm not an angel, Bron, I don't pretend to be, but I can
tell you straight, what you see is what you get.'

A babe magnet is what I see, she thought, thinking of
what Jack said, but I have no idea what you are really like.
I thought you were my friend but I was wrong.

'Can you take me home now, please?'

'Sure,' he said. 'Not a problem.'

CHAPTER FOUR

IT HAD rained for over a week, warm wet rain that soaked the roads and the fields. It came with regular monotony day after day. It was even wearing Bron down and she normally did not let weather bother her.

The constant downpour had made puddles across her lawn. As she made a turn to pull into her parking place she noted that everything looked so sodden and miserable, just how she was feeling inside.

Time had fled by and she had not heard from Jack. She had imagined he would write an explanatory note, even if he did not tell her where he was. The fact that he had not been in touch nagged away at her. Whatever he had done, and he had done sufficient to strangle any love she had left for him, she had imagined he would at least have the decency to let her know he was all right.

It was not like Jack to do something like that, to just disappear, yet how did she know? She had not thought that Jack would abscond with her money and even try to raise capital on their home without telling her. Even so, the mystery of his disappearance would not leave her in peace.

It was the not knowing that got to her, far more than

his actual – and she used a modern expression – *dumping* her. She could cope with that and secretly, if she was honest, that was the least of her worries. She knew she could be happy on her own, that she was a different person now having discovered her confidence once more, and was certainly strong enough to live her life as a single woman.

When she saw a strange car on her drive, her heart gave a leap and then a cold sense of despair rushed over her. She was not expecting anyone – it could only mean trouble. The pessimism was not lost on her. Months ago she would have called it a surprise, and a pleasant one at that, that someone had come to call. This feeling of despair because a stranger had arrived was all as a result of Jack's betrayal.

After pulling up the hood on her lightweight anorak, she left her car and ran to the parked vehicle. The car's windows were steamed up and soaked with raindrops; she tapped lightly on the window. It started to wind down.

'Hello,' she cried. 'Who is it?'

The lisping voice caused her to sink into even deeper melancholy.

'Why it's me, Bron, Marged . . . I'm back!'

The house soon warmed up after Bron switched on the heating. She drew the shutters on the windswept dark night and then made tea. Marged was ensconced in a long rain cape and was going backwards and forwards to the car, bringing in bags and a couple of suitcases.

The tea made, Bron set it up on the occasional table by the side of the fireplace.

She threw a lighted match into the wood and paper and soon the dry wood caught and she was able to put on a small log.

She enjoyed the firelight and often sat just here but, remembering she was not alone, she stood up and turned on some lamps.

There was something different about Marged. As she pulled off the cape to reveal tight jeans and a dark red sweater, Bron thought it was the clothes. She had never seen her cousin wear such modern clothes before. They suited her too. She still had the thick braid of golden hair but there were golden hoop earrings at her ears and a lighter streak of hair went from her hairline and threaded its way down the plait. It was very stylishly done, Bron saw, and obviously by a skilled hair stylist.

Yet it was more than even that; it was in the way she walked and moved. Marged had a self-assurance that she had never before showed. Although she had always been good looking, it had not been apparent on first seeing her, because she seemed so folded into herself, as if she were hiding her attractiveness. Now it was out in the open and the young woman blossomed with confidence. She was more than good looking. Marged was alluring.

She threw herself into the settee, reaching out for the teapot and pouring some in each cup. 'I've had a marvellous time,' she announced after taking a small sip of the brew. 'I would have called you . . . I should have called you, but when I got to Auckland and got the car, I just kept driving. The weather was so bad, I was a bit scared to stop in case the road closed or anything. You can't imagine what it was like getting up here.'

'Oh yes I can,' Bron said mildly. 'You did well to make it up. If I had been driving, believe me, I would have stayed at a lodge or somewhere till daylight.'

'Well . . .' Marged smiled, obviously pleased with herself. 'I'm a big girl now. I did think of telephoning Jack and asking to stay over.' She shrugged. 'But then . . . I wanted to get here.'

Bron was forming the words in her head to tell her cousin that Jack was no longer in Auckland. She did not relish telling Marged the whole sorry story, that Jack had disappeared and that she did not even know where he was. That he had left Auckland in the summer and it was now winter and she still had not heard anything from him. However, before she could speak, Marged started off again. She was talking quickly and with lots of animation and hand waving.

'I went everywhere in South Island, even beyond Christchurch, right to the bottom, then I thought, what the heck, I've got the travelling bug, so I went to Australia. I had such fun. Have you ever been to Melbourne? It's great, my kind of place, not too hot, you know, really cool in every sense of the word. I did Sydney and Brisbane, which I loved, but Melbourne is my kind of town. I might go back. I could settle there. Trouble is, unlike you, I don't have a profession, so getting a visa might be difficult. I mean, what could I do? I've never had a proper job.'

Bron recalled that Marged had done very well at school, getting excellent grades, but she had never taken up a place at sixth form to do A levels. In fact, she had done little with her life. Aunt Lily had the small shop selling sweets and tobacco. It was actually a good business at one time, being near the local cinema and a couple of schools, but then like many small businesses it hit the doldrums. The cinema closed and a huge supermarket opened nearby. It probably just about kept Aunt Lily and Marged and eventually they sold up. That was just before Marged married Denis.

'Didn't you do anything after Denis left?' Bron asked carefully.

'Well, yes, I worked at the supermarket on the till but it was hardly high tech. I need some kind of training.' Marged sighed, showing discontent for the first time since she had arrived.

'I haven't a sponsor for Australia, but I could stay here . . . in New Zealand, I mean. You would sponsor me, I'm sure. Perhaps I could train for something here, or in Auckland. What do you think?'

'I could do that for you but perhaps in England you would be able to get on training courses more easily. What do you have in mind?'

'I don't know,' Marged sighed. 'I'm not desperate for money. Maybe I could buy a little shop. That's what I am good at, dealing with people.'

Although she felt it uncharitable, Bron was surprised to hear that, for the one thing about the old Marged she knew was that she was dreadful with people. She had been sulky and uncommunicative, hardly ever the life and soul of any party. But maybe that was what was different about her now. She had spoken more in the last three quarters of an hour than Bron had ever heard her speak before.

'Perhaps I could buy a dairy or something small like that. I don't know.' She waved her arms. 'I feel as if the world is my oyster and I could do anything but I don't know what. Isn't that strange?' Then after a pause for breath: 'You're very quiet, Bron. Are you OK?'

Ignoring the question for the moment, Bron asked, 'When you stayed with Jack, how did he seem?'

'Jack?' Marged's eyes went round and her full lips pouted. Then she shrugged with indifference. 'Well, Jack was Jack, you know, laid back and funny, just Jack. He's good fun, you know. Why do you ask? Don't tell me he has been up to something? Not your Jack.' She laughed.

'As a matter of fact he has.' Bron tried to steady her voice but there was a tightness about it. Marged's description of Jack seemed so off-centre that it was almost laughable. But then again, perhaps he had behaved differently around her. That almost seemed to confirm in Bron's head that it was she that Jack was up against. Not New Zealand, not home-sickness, just her!

'What?' Marged asked. 'You've gone quite pale, Bron. Are you all right?'

'Not really,' Bron sighed. 'Jack has left me.'

'Left you? Jack? But you were the perfect couple, every-one said so.'

'*Everyone*? I can't imagine who everyone is,' Bron murmured, realizing it was quite an exaggeration, for everyone she knew did not know Marged.

Marged shrugged irritably. 'You know what I mean. Mum and I. Your mother liked Jack.'

'Most women did,' Bron muttered. 'He was the kind of man women liked: friendly, good looking, as you say, laid back. Anyway . . .' Bron stifled another sigh. 'He left. I don't know where he went, he just disappeared.'

Marged's rather plump pink tongue slid out of her mouth, flicking restlessly across her lips. Then she said, 'Rather like Denis. Curious, don't you think, that both our husbands went away without telling us anything?'

That was something that Bron had forgotten. She admit-ted to herself that it was a strange coincidence. They were two cousins both having husbands who deserted them and vanished off the face of the earth. 'Did he take money?' she asked. 'Denis, I mean?'

'He took the takings from the till but he didn't have access to the bank account. You know my mother. She was always a little suspicious about Denis; I don't know why. I used to think it was just her, being like she always was . . .'

'And what was that?' Bron asked, although she was well aware of the answer.

'Possessive,' Marged said, confirming what Bron already knew. 'No one was ever going to be good enough for me in her eyes. She told me to wait for my prince to come. As if!' She sounded unusually bitter. 'Anyway, that's enough about me. I am sorry, Bron, I know what you must be feeling.'

I don't think you do, Bron thought, but she was not going to go down that avenue. Undoubtedly Marged had to have suffered pain and humiliation when Denis left, but it was different for her. After all, there were the years between her and Jack; they had been together a long time, far longer than the two years that Denis and Marged were together. There was a shared past; a time of sacrifice on her part as she supported Jack through his training. It was a coincidence that both cousins had been left by their husbands but there was no deeper link to it.

'What are you going to do?' Marged asked.

'Wait for the time to pass until I can divorce him.' Bron heard the coldness in her voice.

'It's seven years. That's a long time. Unless you hire someone to find him.'

'I'm in no hurry. And I don't feel inclined to pay good money to someone to find Jack. Besides, like the proverbial bad penny, I am sure he will turn up . . . one day. He will want something – half the value of this house, for a start. If he runs out of the money he took I am sure his thoughts will turn to that.'

'So he took your money?' Marged asked, her eyes hot with curiosity. 'How much did he take?'

But Bron was in no mood to talk figures. 'Just say, enough to make it a long time before I have a decent sum in my bank again. He also sold the boat, in spite of the fact that it was in joint names.'

'Oh, Bron, I am really so sorry.'

Yet there was no real feeling in the words, nor did she show any emotion. Staff at school had taken hold of her and given her hugs when they had found out what had happened, yet her cousin did not even take up her hand. Not that Marged had ever been a 'touchy feely' kind of person, but her reaction was so unemotional, as if the sequence of events were nothing at all, just an inconvenient incident in her cousin's life.

The rain had stopped beating against the window panes. Crossing the room and opening the shutters, Bron saw it had stopped raining entirely. The wind had died down too. It gave her an idea. She did not feel like cooking for two; had she been on her own she would have made something simple like beans on toast, yet she felt she could not offer something like that to Marged. After all, the woman had driven all the way up here from Auckland.

'Get your coat,' she announced. 'We'll go to the RSA club for dinner.'

There was no protest from Marged, not even when Bron said they could walk – if it rained someone would give them a lift home – because she felt like a glass of wine.

'Me too,' Marged, who seldom drank anything, agreed.

After the rain there was a lovely ripe scent about everything; even the soil smelt good. The area had been washed clean and everywhere sparkled in the moonlight. After walking for less than five minutes they hit the town, and they wandered along the pavement, past the shuttered shops. The dairy, which was up for sale, was still open and Marged paused to look in through the windows as if considering whether it would be a worthwhile proposition. For her part, Bron thought it was the last thing Marged should do. Not at least until she had tried working in a dairy to see if she liked it. It was a good little business but they opened long hours to make it successful.

There were a good few cars outside the RSA club and when they went inside, several couples greeted Bron in a friendly and casual kind of way. They took a table at the far side of the room and it was Marged who opted to face the room, as if she wanted to watch for someone. There were three selections on the menu and they both opted for the fish, knowing that it would be really good. Their wine came in tall, fat glasses, making for large measures. Bron sipped hers; it was crisp and dry and wonderfully cool. Looking up she saw Marged eagerly scanning the room and realized that she had to be looking for someone in particular.

'He doesn't come here,' she said.

'Who's that?' Marged asked, feigning ignorance.

'Job Tepi.'

'But I wasn't . . .' Her colour deepened, proving her lie. She had to have felt the heat staining her complexion for she gave her familiar shrug, and a little, rather sly smile. 'Well, he is . . . cute.'

Cute. The word was so inappropriate to describe Job Tepi. There was nothing cute about Job Tepi at all. 'I don't see him. Well hardly,' Bron said tightly.

'You don't? I would have thought you would have seen him a lot I mean, he was rather sweet on you.'

'That's ridiculous. The man has a harem of women, and none of them look like a deputy head teacher – more like model of the year.'

'Still . . .' Marged hesitated. 'I sort of got a whiff of something.'

'There was nothing. There never would be anything. We

62

were friendly, but that's all.'

'Well, it's nice that he was your friend,' Marged said, but there was a hint of sarcasm there. 'So why don't you see him any more?'

'I see him in the supermarket sometimes. I never see him socially. In the first place I don't sail at all now, I don't have a boat, and secondly he . . .' Now it was her turn to hesitate. Why was she telling this to Marged? Marged was not the kind of girl one shared confidences with, cousin or not. 'He has a busy life.' She decided on not revealing his involvement with Jack. There would be no point.

'Well, if you're sure, then you would not mind if I flirted a little with him?'

'Flirt with him?' Bron questioned and when Marged did not confirm or deny that's what she meant, added, 'It has nothing to do with me what you do, Marged, but I am a little surprised you would want to – I've never thought of you as flirtatious.'

'It's the new me,' she beamed. 'You know since I've been travelling, I really feel as if I have been reborn into a different body. Now I am really going to have fun. I deserve it, don't you think?'

'You do deserve to have some fun. I would say to you, though, be careful of Job Tepi, he isn't what he seems.'

'What makes you say that? Come on, out with it. You two were so friendly before. Has he upset you? Made a pass?' She made the last three words sound so crude that Bron felt a stirring of anger.

'Of course not,' she protested.

'Is that the problem? I mean that he didn't?' Marged lowered long silky lashes over her eyes, her lips making that perfect little pout that she did so successfully. When Bron did not reply she murmured, almost under her breath, 'Maybe . . .'

'I was thinking it didn't require comment. I've just had my husband walk out on me. Do you really think I want another relationship, and with a man I could never trust?' The words were out before she could stop them. She realized she had revealed far too much. However, the waiter came with their meal and immediately, as if she hadn't eaten in a long time, Marged tucked into her food.

Somehow they got through the food and the small talk and it was time to head back to the house. Some near neighbours offered them a ride and Bron was glad of the distraction. Surprising her, Marged was lively and friendly and chatted more amiably to the strangers than Bron had ever known her do before. Something had happened to Marged while she was away. She was an entirely different person.

When Bron arrived home from school she sat some long moments in the car. She needed the time alone before she faced Marged. Her cousin had been sleeping when she left for school; obviously she had not gone out, for her car was parked on the drive.

The routine that Bron had established was going to erode, she saw that. There had been some compensation in coming home from school and just doing as she wished. A shower, a glass of wine, her evening meal, then perhaps some television or she would read a book. It was dull but it was oddly comforting, a comfort she needed after the shock of Jack's betrayal. Now and again she would have a meal with Ruthie and Adam next door but mainly she liked to spend the time closeted and alone in her home.

Grimacing, she left the car, not bothering to lock it. The house was still and silent, just how she liked it these days.

She called out, 'Marged,' and only her own voice echoed back to her. She saw why when she went into the kitchen; by the kettle was a note from Marged.

'Gone up country with Job.'

Well, she sighed to herself, it seems as if Marged is more resourceful than I thought. Somehow she had contacted Job and of course that was easy. His number was in her personal directory that sat by the telephone. One call had brought him running, so he had to be attracted in some way to Marged. Well, she mused, plugging in the kettle to make a cup of tea, she was his type. He seemed to like blondes, although not usually blondes like Marged. She shrugged. 'Who cares!' she said out loud.

A light tap on the door drew her back to the hall. Ruthie was standing in the porch. 'Come and have a cuppa,' Bron said. In spite of wanting to enjoy her solitude, it was always a pleasure to see Ruthie, who always had some lively and interesting chatter and who often drove away her depression. She looked like an older version of Job, with her long black hair and those curious dark-green speckled eyes. That she must have been a stunner when younger went without saying. She could still turn heads now.

'What about her?' Ruthie said, following Bron back into the kitchen.

'Who?'

'Marged, that's who. You know she called up our Job, asked him to take her up to Ninety Mile. I mean, the nerve of that girl.'

'Oh,' Bron said quietly, and then slid the note over to Ruthie. 'She did not say she had *asked* him.'

Ruthie glanced at the note. 'Well, she did. I mean, I'm all for female emancipation but I think that's going too far. She hardly knows Job.'

'All the better to get to know him,' Bron answered smoothly.

'Look, Bron, I know you and Job haven't seen eye to eye for a while but he isn't a bad bloke, you know.'

'I'm sure he isn't, Ruthie. I think Marged has rather taken a fancy to him.'

'You can say that again. I know she's had a hard time and that she's your cousin but I . . . sorry, I think I'd better shut up.' She took her cup of tea, curling her hands around the beaker as if for warmth.

'You don't like her?' Bron said, more to show Ruthie it was all right to have an opinion than to want to pry. 'You can *not* like her, Ruthie. You don't have to like her because she's my cousin. She's an odd girl, although not a bad girl. It's her upbringing, really. Her mother was so possessive. She never let her have her teens to herself, if you know what I mean. I mean, they used to go everywhere together; it wasn't natural. So now perhaps Marged feels she wants to make up for what she missed. Kick over the traces, if you like.'

'Yes,' Ruthie said but doubtfully. 'I suppose I can see that. But I was annoyed when he told me and I told him so.'

'And what did he say?'

'Told me to mind my own business, of course. You know Job's not one to bottle things up. Straight out with it, that's him.'

When Ruthie had left after staying for about half an hour, Bron, unsettled for no reason that she could analyze, set about wiping down the units in the kitchen, then after making a sandwich wandered into the living room. She switched on the computer and when it was booted, perused her e-mails. There were a couple from friends in England and Australia. She read and answered them all. The last one was from an address she did not recognize. For a moment she idled on the mouse, wondering whether to delete it, then curiosity winning, she clicked on open.

She stared at it for a long time, blinking, shook her head and then re-read the message:

I'm sorry – I had to get away – you can guess where I am in the UK. If you think about it you will come up with the place. I'm OK – just short of money. Once things are settled with me, I want you to sell the house. You can come over here if you want or stay there. It's over between us. I know you, Bron, and you wouldn't want me back, would you? Perhaps you can get a valuation for the house. E-mail me back so I will have some idea of the kind of money I can look forward to. Jack.

CHAPTER FIVE

PERHAPS, she thought, she had come to the wrong place, taken a wrong turn. She went around the block a couple of times. The office of the lawyer that Job Tepi had taken her to was not where she thought it had been.

In the end she went to the post office and used a telephone book to look them up.

There was no one of that name listed.

She thought, I'm going mad, I've dreamt it all and one day I will wake up and see it is a terrible dream. A huge lorry manoeuvring the street, past some roadworks, convinced her she was well and truly awake. She gagged on the diesel fumes emanating from it.

There was a café nearby; she went in, closing the door on the sound of drills and traffic. The girl behind the counter gave her a welcoming smile.

'It's terrible out there but it will soon be finished. What would you like, ma'am?'

She ordered coffee and a piece of cake. She did not really feel like eating but her stomach was empty and she felt a little dizzy.

Last night she had barely slept. Marged had not come home, nor had she bothered to call or leave a message.

However, by seven Bron was on the road to Whangarei and called school to apologize for her absence.

'Something has come up. I have to deal with it today,' she told the headteacher, who was sympathetic.

'Take as long as you need, Bron,' she said kindly.

Only now did she realize that her journey was not only wasted but foolish. A telephone call would have sufficed to confirm that Job Tepi had been up to something. The lawyer was obviously a phoney, the affidavit she had signed probably not even legal.

She slid a piece of cake into her mouth, the sweetness made her head spin for a fraction of a second. The coffee was better.

For a long moment she stared into the street, trying to blank out the anger and the schemes that were helter-skeltering into her mind. What was Tepi up to? Why had he lied? Obviously there was something in all this that would be to his benefit but what could that be? Did he have a hold on Jack? Was there more going on than what he had hinted at?

When she gained some control she went and found where she had parked her car and set off home. The drive, peaceful and quiet, calmed her somewhat. It was therapeutic and gave her time to think too. By the time she reached the house, she had let the anger fade and a coldness take its place. Cold was better. It enabled her to think what she would do.

She had been angry with Jack and then with Job Tepi, both men linked by a common agenda, but she was not going to let either of them get the better of her. Jack could sing for his share of the house. Unless she had some answers and Jack came to her through a real lawyer, she was going to do nothing.

As to selling the house, she had no intention of selling the thing she had managed to hold on to. Besides, she loved the house and her life, and she was not going to give up either without a real fight. There was something so special about the old colonial property, with its veranda and gardens and huge comfortable rooms. It was redolent of an atmosphere that appealed to each of her senses; it was the history, the people who had lived before her. Settlers who had carved out a new life. She was not going to give it up, no matter if she had to beggar herself.

Marged was back. Marged was another interference and one she could well do without.

She said, the words ringing out falsely, 'Sorry I didn't call, but you know how it is.'

'No, how is it?' Bron asked, still retaining her cool aloofness.

'You know,' Marged said, playing at being rather cute, 'you forget . . . *everything*!'

'I've never had the pleasure of forgetting *everything*,' Bron said tartly. 'Anyway, Marged, what you do is your own business.'

The blonde girl came closer, leaning a rounded hip against the worktop as Bron put on the coffee maker. 'You're not . . . *jealous*?'

'Of what precisely would I be jealous?'

'Me and Job,' she lisped. 'Our being together.'

'Are you . . . *together*?' Bron asked, then went on: 'And if you are, I am not jealous. I told you, Marged, Job Tepi means nothing to me, either now, previously, or in the future.'

'OK, that's fine, then. Let me make your coffee. Did you have a hard day? You look stressed.'

'I did have a hard day, Marged, and thank you, I'll be in the sitting room.'

She flopped on the settee. It was good to feel some measure of control coming back into her life. There was going to be no manipulation of her from now on, she was going to be in charge of things. The first thing she had to do was to find where Jack was. She had an idea the place he mentioned was the village in Wales where they had gone for all their holidays. It was their bolthole. She had gone there as a child and had taken Jack. He had loved it as she had. That could be the only place where he would go. The hint was there and so she would go and find him and confront him once and for all.

After she had done that he would be out of her life because she would finish it.

Marged came bustling into the room carrying the coffee jug, and with two beakers threaded through the fingers of her other hand. She placed the stuff down on the occasional table and then went back to the kitchen, returning with milk and sugar.

'There,' she announced pleasantly, 'help yourself.'

Bron poured the coffee into a beaker for herself, took it up and managed a short sip before saying. 'There's something I have to do, Marged. I have to go away. I don't mind if you stay at the house but would you be all right on your own?'

'Well, of course, but what do you mean?'

'It seems that Jack is in the UK.'

'He is?' she queried, surprised.

'I had an e-mail. I have to go and confront him.'

'What does he want? I mean, will you make up? Perhaps you would stay over there with him.'

'I definitely won't do that, Marged. This is my home now

and I intend to come back as soon as possible. There will be no reconciliation; Jack has done too much for me to ever forgive him.'

'He has behaved pretty despicably,' Marged said. She tried to sound genuinely sympathetic but Bron heard the insincerity in her tone. However, she brushed it to one side. It did not matter that Marged wasn't totally interested in her problems. She knew she could never be a real friend to Marged and it made things easier if her cousin felt more or less the same.

'But what will you do about your job?'

'I don't know how they will feel about giving me a leave of absence. It might be difficult and if it is, I can't help it. I have to do this. I have to confront Jack and end it all once and for all.'

'How are you fixed financially? I mean, Jack took some money, didn't he?'

'Yes, he did. But there is still my rainy day money.'

'Rainy day money? What's that?'

'Well, my mother left a good few premium bonds. I had to cash them in but I immediately put the cash back into new Bonds. I can cash those in. I don't know why I did not put the money into joint names like everything else . . . a forgetful moment when I was depressed over my parents' deaths, but a fortunate one, you might say.'

'I would say. So it will be enough to pay your fare?'

'Mm, and expenses. After that I'm cleaned out but I need to do this.'

'I can see that. I'll look after the house for as long as you like. Actually, I was talking to Job about work and he said he might be able to find me a job in one of his hotels. There's a little shop, selling gifts. He said I could work there part-time till I find something or decide what I want to do. I think I'll take up his offer. I'm also going on a computer course; he thinks he knows where I can do that.'

'That sounds great. My being away will give you time to establish yourself and to think seriously about what you want to do.'

'Yes, I think so. I really will look after your home, Bron,' she said, then let her eyes travel the room. 'I just love this house. It's perfect.'

'So do I, and believe me, Marged, I intend to keep it.'

It all took longer than she had anticipated to arrange her departure. Firstly there was school; however, they were, as it turned out, the least of her problems. They were sympathetic and supportive but needed to find someone to replace Bron temporarily while she was away. It was not the kind of job anyone could do. Various negotiations had to be gone through but eventually, through a swap here and a person there, a senior teacher from another school agreed to come. She was hoping to move to deputy head, therefore the experience offered by the temporary assignment, would be good.

Another e-mail had come from Jack, similar to the first and making the same demands. She must sell the house and let him have this share. Angrily she fired off a reply informing him that she was negotiating and would let him know something soon. As soon as she could she would fly over and see him and they could finish everything there and then.

The one thing she did not want him to know was that she was going to confront him. He had to think that everything was going just as he wanted. Surprise would be a good element in knocking him off balance. Hard as she tried, she just could not reconcile the Jack he had become with the

Jack she had known. That Jack had been laid back and friendly, never much bothered about money or possessions. He had changed beyond all recognition. Of course, he had been drinking too much and that might have had some effect on his change of personality, but the essence of him seemed no longer there and that was what she could not understand.

Marged was out most evenings; the situation that Job had found for her required her to work four nights a week. Bron did not think the girl was too pleased but she went along with it. On a Thursday evening she attended a computer class, so Bron hardly saw her. Mostly at weekends Marged went out and Bron assumed she did so with Job, although she never actually confirmed that she was going out with him. Oddly, neither did Ruthie make any comment about Marged and Job. However, given how Ruthie felt about Marged, it was probably as well.

Two days before she was due to leave, the bell sounded on the front door. She crossed the hall, expecting Ruthie, although she knew she usually rang the bell and then came in. She threw open the door and was surprised to see it was not Ruthie but her brother.

Job looked – and the words came swimming into her head, making her feel a little dizzy – devastatingly attractive. He was wearing a suit of dark blue shiny material, a white silk shirt and a pale blue tie. There was an air of business about him that she had never noticed before. Of course, she had rarely seen the man of business because when they had met it had been socially or down at the marina, when casual dress was the required style.

The feelings he had provoked made her ask sharply, 'What do you want?'

He raised a dark eyebrow at her. 'I need to talk to you,' he said.

'Well, I don't have the need to listen,' she said, going to close the door. His foot prevented her from slamming it; she looked down, her mouth twisting cynically. 'Are you doorstepping me, Job? Is this what you do to your clients when they don't pay up?'

'What are you talking about?' he asked. 'Listen, Bron, I will talk to you whether you want me to or not. I'll even shout through the door if you don't let me in.'

'I'm sure you would,' she spat. 'You would really like to make me uncomfortable.'

'Of course I wouldn't. You can't see it but I do have your best interests at heart.'

'Oh yes? Is that why you took me to the phoney lawyer?'

'The phoney what?' He looked genuinely puzzled.

'I went there. The building was empty.'

'You went where?'

'To Whangarei.'

'Let me inside, Bron.'

What could he do to her? He would not physically harm her. He probably had other people who did things like that. What he wanted she could not imagine and she was curious in spite of her own misgivings. He was a liar and a cheat and not particular about legality, yet still she wanted to know what he had to say. She opened the door, stepped aside and let him come in.

Leading the way to the living room, she went and stood behind the sofa as if in need of protection, but really needing something to lean against in case the dizziness came back.

'They moved to a new office building. If you had asked me I would have told you.'

'They weren't in the phone book.'

'They changed the name of the firm.'

'How convenient,' she sneered.

'Not really, very practical. But I'm not here to talk about them. Why are you going to the UK, Bron?'

She gasped. Then realized that Marged must have told him. 'No one is supposed to know,' she said.

'What are you afraid of? Do you think I'd warn him? You must be joking. You must also be a fool to think Jack is in the UK, Bron. He isn't there, I'm certain of it.'

'Oh, really, and why are you so *certain* of it?'

'Actually, perhaps certain is the wrong word. It's a gut feeling. I don't get Jack going to the UK and then wanting to negotiate money. It doesn't make sense. He would stay here if he wanted to do that.'

'None of it makes sense,' she retaliated angrily. 'And none of it is your damned business.'

'Sure it is. Jack owes me too – he owes me a lot of money.'

'Well, that's your problem.'

'I could make it yours,' he said, 'if I had a mind.'

'That sounds like a threat, Job, and I do hope you are not threatening me.'

'You know I'm not. Bron, I think you should stay where you are and not leave this house. Suppose Jack came back while you are away.'

'Are you afraid for Marged?'

He pushed his hands into his trouser pockets, rocking on the balls of his feet. A shaft of light came sneaking in through the window. It highlighted the polished bronze of his complexion. He had been her friend and now he was someone that she suspected.

'I imagine Marged can look after herself,' he said at last. 'But you can't. You are going on some wild goose chase and

I don't know why.'

'It's very simple, I want it over with. I want Jack to know he can't push me around.'

'Let a lawyer do that.'

'I need to do it myself.'

'I don't trust it, any of it.'

'Well, it takes one to know one.'

'Look, Bron, I don't blame you for being bitter. I should have told you what was going on but look at it from my point of view, won't you? Suppose I had told you. Do you think you would have believed me? Jack I'm sure could have convinced you otherwise. Besides, I didn't see it as my place to come between husband and wife.'

'You know what I think, Job, I think you exploited him.'

He folded his arms across his middle; only the slight pulsating of a muscle to the side of his mouth showed her that he was feeling more than a little tense.

'And just how did I do that?'

'You loaned him money and you knew he was gambling, or was it that he was gambling with you?'

'Not with me, gambling is for mugs.'

'And you had nothing to do with his . . . his addiction?'

He looked away, dropping his arms. They hung at his side limply, and a faint flush stained his high cheekbones.

'I'm waiting for an answer, Job. How come someone usually so articulate can't think of . . . shall I call it an excuse?'

'I took him to a club. I own the building. I don't own what goes on there but I know the bloke that runs it. Sure I felt guilty about it, but how was I to know he had an addictive personality? Did you know he had an addictive personality?'

Not until recently, she thought but she could not say the

words. However, she did shake her head showing that she had no idea. And maybe Jack did not have an addictive personality, he was just sucked in, an innocent abroad, but that was lying to herself, she knew that. Jack was no little innocent.

'He was terribly homesick, he changed a lot, and homesickness can make you do the most stupid things.'

Job's shoulders tightened, his chin jutting slightly. 'No one made him come to my country and no one made him stay. He should have got a one-way ticket home if he didn't like us.'

'Well, that's rather childish,' she muttered.

'What do you mean?'

'I mean your taking it personally that he was homesick. That he couldn't settle here.'

'I wasn't doing that. I meant there was nothing making him stay here. Only maybe you were doing that. You settled down here, you're successful. A bit hard to live up to, don't you think?'

'So I'm to blame for doing a good job. That's rich and patronizing too. Maybe it's my entire fault, all of it. Only thing wrong with that, Job, I wasn't making him stay. I offered to go back. I didn't want to but at least I offered. If you want to ameliorate your guilt and push it on me do it, but get your damned facts right.' She took a deep breath, feeling the anger steam itself into nothing. 'Anyway, none of this matters, I'm going to find him and I'm going to sort it out.'

'And we're back to the start of this. I think you're making a big mistake. I don't think you'll find him in England.'

'He is there. I know it for a fact.'

'Oh yes, and how do you know? Have you spoken to him?' Job's eyes narrowed suspiciously.

'Not exactly.'

'I think I can guess. You had an e-mail from him.'

Her heart gave a jolt, and the hint of suspicion started to nag at her mind. He knew *something*, this man she had thought was her friend. He knew more than he was saying.

'There's no point in denying it, I can tell by looking at your face. Listen, e-mails can come from anywhere. I think Jack is here in New Zealand and he is just luring you away and then . . .'

'What then?'

'He'll take over this house.'

'Why would he do that if he was so unhappy here?' She made her tone sarcastic but really there was now more than suspicion, there was a frisson of fear as well. Job was smarter than she had given him credit for, craftier even. He was using his own cunning to work out what Jack might do. Yet surely Jack wanted only the money, not tenancy of the house?

'Money, ownership, the ability to have charge of events. Jack was a man who liked being in charge; the trouble was he did not have the necessary qualifications to make it all happen. Listen, Bron, I like you, you're a decent person, but where this thing is concerned you're in over your head.'

She turned from him, shambling across the sitting room. She made for an armchair, lowering herself into it wearily. Her legs felt weak; the possibility that Jack would be that cunning had never occurred to her. And yet a man who had stolen money from their joint account, who had sold their boat from under her nose, then that man was not the man she had married. He was someone she did not know any more and someone that would be capable of things she had no imagination for.

Aware that Job had now come across to her, she did not

even bother to look up but sat quietly watching the dust motes cavort in a ragged sunbeam. His argument had frightened her, weakened her resolve to do things her way.

'At least let me track the e-mails,' Job said at last. 'Let me prove it to you.'

Tiredly she nodded, pulling herself out of the chair and going to the computer. She clicked on to the server and then left him to it.

He came to find her; she was just standing in the kitchen, running the tap and staring down into the kitchen sink, watching swirls of water as it made its way down the hole.

'Bron,' he said. She turned to face him. He looked confused. She had never seen him looking like that. He had said Jack was in control, but generally so was he.

'I owe you an apology.'

'You do?'

'Those e-mails came from the UK.'

She wanted to say told you so but she held the words inside her. The heavy weight was pressing her down. Although he could not know it, Job Tepi, with his idea that Jack was still in New Zealand, had given her a crazy kind of hope. She could sort something out. Now that the truth was confirmed, she realized it was going to be difficult. She had to take the hard road, go to the UK, see Jack and have it out with him.

'I still think you should not go. To hell with him. Get another lawyer if you don't trust mine, just don't give him an inch. He could have had a mate send those e-mails, there's no proof they came from him.'

'I don't think that is possible. The friends we have in the UK were our friends; they would not let Jack do something so despicable. Oh, you can look at me like that, but these are genuine friends, Job. Know what they are?'

He stared right into her eyes, his face immobile. 'Think what you like about me, Bron, but don't just ignore what I say. Give it some consideration.'

'Jack and I were married for seven years. We were together three years before that. I can't let go on ten years just like it was nothing. I have to confront him.'

'He might not even be there.'

'I think he is. I want to see him.'

'You want him back?' Job Tepi's eyes widened.

'That isn't your business.'

'If you do then you'd better sell up and go over there. I tell you straight he is in big trouble if he comes back here.'

'What do you mean?' She straightened her shoulders, facing him eye to eye. 'A moment ago you were sure he was in New Zealand, now you tell me he would be in big trouble if he came back. You have to make your mind up. Liars should always be consistent.' She was not going to be the victim in this. She was not going to be intimidated by him or anyone else. 'I don't think he would have anything to fear. I would persuade him to go to the police, and they would soon sort these people out. Or are you these people?'

'Don't be stupid, Bron. Of course I'm not. I told you he owes me money but that is nothing' – he snapped his fingers – 'to what he owes others. Believe me, Bron, these are not understanding people. They are bad news. And as to the police, well they won't do you much good. Jack was a fool, Bron, and I think at the bottom of you, you understand that. As to his not coming back here, well, that is just what he might do but I doubt it very much. If he did he would offer them the house and get off the hook. That's why he would come back. But that depends on his *wanting* to be here, and he doesn't want to be here, does he? He doesn't

81

intend to pay anyone, all he intends to do is rip you off and you are going to let him do it. That scenario is if he is in the UK. If he isn't, then he has to get this house anyway, to pay them off. Wherever he is hiding they will find him, Bron, of that you can be sure.'

It hurt to hear these things. She knew it was probably true. She did not know Jack and the more Job talked about him, the more the reality tore into her newly gained self-esteem. He probably saw her as weak and feeble; she had to bite back somehow.

'What are you doing with Marged?' It came out and she had not even been aware that the question was lurking in her mind. How was that going to show him that she was strong? It was revealing a side of her that only proved his thesis that she was weak and silly and helpless. Job folded his arms across his chest.

'None of your business,' he said, but there was a hint of a smile.

'It is my business. Don't fool with her, Job. She's not as smart as she seems. She led a very sheltered life.'

'I wonder if your concern is for her or for you.'

'What do you mean?' Her heart gave a little jolt. It was a warning. Don't go there, her mind urged. Change this conversation quickly. Get him out of the house and get on with what is important.

'What I mean is, why do you care what I do with Marged? Oh and don't give me that sheltered existence excuse – that is junk and you know it. Marged is not as naïve as she pretends.'

'So, not only do you know all about Jack, you also know all about Marged. How does it feel up there in that lofty kingdom where you know so much about everything?'

'It feels fine. People are my livelihood, Bron. I make it my business to understand them, that's why I am successful. I even understand you.'

'In your dreams you do. Anyway, I have to make arrangements now so if you have finished . . .'

He strolled towards her and she backed away. Moving along the sink until her back rested against the refrigerator, she had moved herself into a corner.

Job stopped within feet of her. He put out a hand and placed it on her shoulder. There was a feeling like a sizzle of electricity that ran up her arm. This is madness, she thought. This man is not to be trusted!

'Bron, I've advised you what to do but do your own thing if you must. Where will you go? Where is this special place he mentions?'

Suddenly it became clear: he wanted to know where Jack was. This was all a ploy; he was in cahoots with the people who were looking for him. That was it and she was stupid for not realizing it sooner. It was all a game to him; trick and trickery, mirrors and deceit. This was what he was anxious about – where Jack was.

'Our old home town, that is where he will be,' she said.

He smiled a genuine smile that showed the brilliant white of his teeth. 'That is the special place that you know, is it?' he murmured.

'It's a pub. We used to go there when we were students. The Black Bull. It's a folk pub, or was. You know, they had folk music. I used to do a gig there now and then.'

'You did?' His eyes were so black now, the chips of green hardly visible. They were wide and open and she stared into their unfathomable depths. It was impossible to see where the iris ended and the pupil began. 'So it would be very special,' he murmured. 'Especially to you. How come you never carried on with your singing?'

'What has that to do with anything?'

'I just wondered. Perhaps Jack didn't like it. But if the Black Bull is such a special place, the place where you used to sing, then I guess I am wrong.'

'You are right, you are wrong.' She felt the red burning against her cheekbones and only hoped that the heat she felt had not manifested itself in colour. She hated lying but if he knew where she was going, who was to say he would not tell the men to whom Jack owed money? She did not doubt that they would be capable of following her there. He gave out a broad hint that these people were ruthless and dangerous. For some strange reason he did not want her to suffer for what Jack had done but that did not make him *her* friend. He would use her to get to Jack.

'Maybe I won't go.' She managed a shrug. 'I'm beginning to think you are right. Why should I be the one to run to him? It isn't as if I've done anything wrong.' Even to her own ears, her voice sounded convincing. 'The one thing I don't want to lose is this house. I don't care if I lose Jack, in fact, I've lost him already.' That was true. One thing she did know for sure was that she would never take Jack back, even if that was what he wanted. She was convinced Jack's only motive for wanting to see her was financial. If he had even a spark of love for her she did not think he would have done what he did. Silence hung between them; Job put his hands in his trouser pockets, ballooning the soft material.

'You do whatever it is you have to do, Bron. Just don't forget that if you need me, I'm here for you.'

He left then, quietly and swiftly, the door closing softly behind him causing a shiver of apprehension to feather her spine. Was it that he knew she was lying? It was not the attitude of someone who had got what he wanted. And what about her, how did she feel about his abrupt departure? For someone who had wanted him to leave the moment he arrived, it was odd she should feel bereft.

She was a mess. Running a hand through her hair, she tugged the ends, as if this would force some positive feelings into her. What would she do? The idea of leaving well alone, of doing what she had told Job she would do, was warming. The idea of now flying to the UK was now abhorrent to her. The former was the wisest course of action. So she would not have closure quickly, it would come one day and perhaps sooner than she thought. Damn Job Tepi. He had turned her positive attitude into indecisiveness.

CHAPTER SIX

IT WAS a balmy midsummer afternoon. Pleasantly warm, with a light breeze drifting in from the Irish Sea perfuming the air. The log cabin complex was open but it was not busy. Too early for the school holidays.

Going directly to the office, she was glad to see it was still open. There was a brass bell on the desk; Jack had always called it the 'brass tit' in his irreverent way. 'Ring the brass tit, Bron,' he would always say. 'You know how you like to do it.'

'You do it, you're the tit man,' she would respond, but then hit the bell hard with the palm of her hand. Now she merely tapped it.

Ellen Jones, or Ellen the Cabins as she was known locally, came out of the office. She was a pretty woman, in her late fifties, with long curling black hair and the true blue eyes of a Celt.

'Bronwen, *pnawn da.*' Ellen came around the counter, drawing Bron to her ample bosom. 'I thought I would never see you again, *cariad*, how are you?'

'I'm fine, Ellen. You look as wonderful as ever.' Bron drew back; the prickling of unease was there at the base of her spine. 'Isn't Jack here?'

'Jack?' Ellen rolled her eyes. 'Your Jack? Cheeky bugger, Jack, I haven't seen him since you two went overseas. Why, Bron, have you lost him?'

Bron booked the cabin for four nights. The one they had both liked was available. It was close to the river and they had loved to lie in bed listening to the water tripping over the stones. There was just the one bedroom but a comfortable lounge with a sofa bed and integral kitchen. It was cosy but once inside and on her own, her mood plummeted into dark depths.

It seemed as if Job Tepi had been right. Jack was out to trick her, yet the e-mail had originated from the UK so he must be in the country . . . *somewhere!*

Jack had said he would meet her here but had not said he would *be* here. There was a world of difference. He could be in town now or on his way. She had replied to the e-mail with dates. It was perfectly feasible that he had decided not to come until she was here. She was being pessimistic and it was not her way. She had sent him flight details. He would arrive tomorrow.

She had stopped on the way and bought a small quiche and some salad; she prepared her evening meal and took a glass of white wine from the bottle she had brought.

After dinner she watched the light fading over the mass of Snowdon, then took a stroll around the site and down by the river before it went really dark, arriving back at the cabin in blue dusk.

She was tired; it had been a long day and the tension had not helped. She lay in bed and listened to the silence before drifting off to sleep. There was, she believed, no silence as magical as a Welsh one.

It was as black as the hobs of hell when she woke up. She lay, listening to the steady thrum of her heart. She could see nothing yet something had wakened her. There was a faint scratching. She listened, her ears working on full power – if it was a mouse she knew she would die. It was ridiculous for a grown woman to be terrified of a little creature like a mouse but she could not help it. She had always intended to get help for it but had never plucked up the courage. Someone had told her they got you to pet the things and the idea turned her stomach. If she put her foot on the floor, suppose it encountered the rounded back of the mouse? But it was more than scratching, it was the latch and no mouse would ever spend its time chewing on a latch.

Nervously, Bron slid out of bed and fumbled for the switch. Her hand encountered the lamp and sent it crashing to the wooden floor. Finding the flex, she slid her hand up it until she found the base, then straightened it and felt for the switch. Her fingers closed around the hard knob, she pressed and the room was filled with a dull pinkish light. The scratching had stopped. She crept across the room, reached the window and folded back the curtain. The sky was awash with stars and a huge moon hung right outside, illuminating the trees and the grass, making the green seem grey.

There was no one outside. If she was back home she would have suspected a mischievous possum but there were no possums in Wales as far as she knew. It could be a fox – but would a fox swing on a latch? Who knew what an impish cub would do? There was nothing human out there. Her overwrought imagination was getting to her. Had it been Jack he would have knocked on the door or tapped on the window. Jack would not have the sense or skill to try and open the door with an implement. He just did not have that kind of brain. Jack was not a DIY man by any stretch of the imagination.

Pulling the curtains back together, she went back into the bedroom, closing the door behind her. Once in bed she felt a little uneasy. There was nothing to be frightened about yet the fear persisted. For the first time in years, she left the light on and eventually fell back to sleep.

In the morning her head felt clearer. Jack would come, it was in his interest to talk to her. He could do nothing about the house in New Zealand without her signature. The lawyer, or whatever he was, who now held the deeds, would not give them to Jack. She was sceptical of Job Tepi and she knew she would never entirely trust him again, but oddly she believed he would not instruct them to give Jack the deeds. If that was what he wanted then he would have dealt with Jack direct. Job had his own agenda with her errant husband.

The weather was perfect. Warm but not too hot, the sun high in the sky, and she had a pair of stout walking shoes. She would head for the hills rather than the beach. They had a favourite walk, it would take the better part of a day but she was better doing that than waiting tensely around the cabin for Jack to arrive. Besides, it would send a signal to Jack, if he did arrive that day, that she was not at his beck and call. It might just teach him a lesson. Although she suspected Jack was beyond any teaching on her part.

It was a straight road but gradually getting steeper; it was the worst part of the walk, and the hard tarmac did little for easing the legs. On either side were fields full of plump and contented sheep and one large house that had a commanding view over the mountains and the bay. She had always loved that house and dreamt of owning it. It was an unrealistic dream but it had never done her any harm.

Close to the top, the road narrowed. Thick trees grew now on either side, and there was a turn to the left and then the road went flat. There were no fences and the sheep wandered from one side of the road to the other. From up there she could look down on the whole of the bay. The sea was very blue, the small white horses looking like curly cotton clouds.

Just before a stile that she needed to take, there was a group of dolman stones, the burial grounds of ancient Celtic tribes. She paused for a moment and listened to the silence. That was what she loved, the perfect silence when even the lightest of breezes carried no sound at all.

After climbing the stile, she took the slate path until it gave way to open countryside. To her far left twin lakes lay still and grey in the valley of green hills that were like the round thrusting breasts of an ancient tribal goddess. The air was fresh and pure; she felt it cleansing her pores, filling her with goodness. Pausing, she looked up towards the gate to where she had to climb; it was a long way off but she had the urge to get there and get there fast. The pleasure to be gained from the view on the other side she knew would be worthwhile.

Concentrating on reaching the gate that hung between two tall rocks, she was unaware of anyone else being on the path. She did not pause to look back – something she had always done in the past – but plodded on. As she neared the gate the climb got steeper but she felt fit enough to do it without any trouble. There was a rush of something, like a sudden bad-tempered blast from the wind and then a pain and then . . . nothing.

CHAPTER SEVEN

MARGED could not sing; it was something she was miserable about. She liked music, liked to sing too, but only to herself. She had not been able to tell that she sung flat until Bron, then fifteen, had asked her, *'Is it painful to sing that song?'*

'No, why?' she had asked.

'Because it's painful to listen to.'

She had always been envious of Bronwen. Clever and pretty Bronwen who had lots of friends and plenty of freedom. It was when her cousin said that, that envy turned to hatred.

Now she felt happy; she loved her cousin's house. There was a mellow beauty about its colonial style. It was a comfortable house and one that was imbued with a cosy friendliness that appealed to Marged. She had never experienced that before – now and again at Bronwen's mother's place she had, but she had never indulged and wallowed in the atmosphere. There was always her mother with her to dampen her spirit.

This is what I am meant for, she thought, this is me. This house, this location – and then there was Job Tepi. He was by far the most thrilling man she had ever met. It was delightful too, for she had taken him off her cousin. In spite of her protestations to the contrary, Marged knew that Bronwen fancied him like mad. It was in the way she looked at the man when they were talking. She had seen them whispering at the Burns Night party; she knew what her cousin hoped for. But now it was to be hers. It was she who had ensnared Job Tepi.

For someone with little experience I don't do so badly, she mused. She had ensnared Jack but he had been far too easy, almost as easy as Denis had been. Instinctively she knew what men liked, how to talk to them and importantly when not to say anything at all. It was that air of mystery that she had that drew them to her. It was that too that would keep them coming back for more. Just like Job Tepi.

She checked her watch. He would be here soon. The table was set, the meal cooked. How he had eagerly accepted her invitation to dinner. He had cleared his diary in an instant.

'I really want to thank you,' she had lisped, 'for helping me get the job, for being there for me.' Her eyes had widened. He had been putty in her hands.

The bell tinkled out, and she took her time crossing the wooden floor. There had been a storm earlier and it was chilly. She had lit the fire in the main room and, as she went by she could not help noticing how it added to the seductive atmosphere. Low lights, soft music, flickering flames. It could only get better.

Job looked gorgeous, no other word for it. He was wearing a dark brown lightweight suit of some very expensive material, and his silk shirt, open at the neck, was dark cream, highlighting his polished complexion. The cologne he imbued was spicy, not too overpowering, but just right. That was how he was, she mused, just right.

'Hello, Marged,' he murmured, giving her a swift appraisal. The soft blue sweater she wore emphasized the swell of her breasts. Her breasts were fuller than Bronwen's, and her waist smaller, accentuated by the wide tan leather belt she wore. Her black pencil skirt rested just on her knee and she wore high-heeled shoes. The shoes, bright scarlet patent, were Bronwen's – she was lucky they had the same size feet. The rest of Bronwen's things did not fit her at all. However, the single strand of pearls was Bronwen's too. They had belonged to her mother, Marged's aunt, a woman of happy disposition, Marged remembered, and who was more like a friend to her daughter rather than the gaoler that her own mother was.

Job smiled and squeezed her hand, and then he kicked off his shoes before coming in. Ah, she had forgotten that. Who cared anyway? It was a stupid custom and the scarlet shoes made her legs look too good for her to take them off. Oh no, these were very seductive shoes. He was polite enough not to mention the shoes; she liked that about him.

To her question as to what he would like to drink, he asked for a beer. She had made it her business to find out what he liked to drink. His favourite beer was cooling in the refrigerator.

'I'm driving, Marged, so just the one beer.'

'Oh, what a shame. I thought you were staying at the flat?'

The flat was actually two rooms above the hotel. When one of the staff had taken her on a tour she had shown Marged where the boss lived. It consisted of a comfortable lounge and a bedroom. Quite small and impersonal but then he did not stay there permanently. No one knew where his house was but there was speculation that it was fantastic. There was rumour too of a luxurious apartment by the marina in Auckland but no one knew anything for certain. It was odd really that no one knew, they were living in such a small community that hardly anyone had secrets. Job had secrets, though, and that made him exciting and *dangerous*.

Obviously his bitch of a sister would know whether he had a house or not, but Marged quickly realized that she was never going to be friends with Ruthie. For some reason Ruthie did not like her; Marged had never given her cause for such dislike but she sensed it.

Of course, Ruthie was Bronwen's friend. Maybe his sister had thoughts of Bronwen dumping Jack and taking off with Job. Fat chance, Marged thought, as she poured the amber-coloured beer into a crystal glass. She was not going to give *him* an ordinary tumbler.

For herself she took a glass of wine, again poured into one of Bronwen's best crystal glasses. The table was laid with silver and the really good china. She was familiar with the stuff – it had been Bronwen's mother's and on special occasions it was always wheeled out and used.

'Have you heard from Bron?' he asked as she handed him his drink. This was not the first time he had asked. It irritated her but she smiled up at him.

'My, you seem so anxious about Bron. She's very self-sufficient, you know, and no, I haven't heard from her. Not even a phone call, but she didn't say that she would telephone or anything.'

'You think she's self-sufficient?'

'Of course. Don't you?'

94

But he made no answer, merely raising one of his dark, well-shaped brows inquisitively.

'Bronwen has always been confident,' Marged said. 'Her parents adored her, you know, they gave her everything she wanted.'

'I would have thought that would have made her a spoiled brat, but she isn't that,' Job defended, albeit in a smooth, unruffled tone of voice.

'Do you like her?' Marged asked. It was not what she really wanted to say. What she actually wanted to say was, Do you fancy her? But she sensed that would put his back up.

'Of course I like her. What is not to like about Bron? She's kind and pleasant.'

'Not all the time – but you wouldn't know that. She can be pretty spiteful when she wants to be. She was very spiteful to me when we were little, always the superior one.' Marged weighed him. No sign of irritation, not even a faint flicker. Nor did he come to the defence of her cousin. Emboldened, she went on, carefully listing, in her whispery voice, all the little digs that Bronwen had got in at her. The last thing she said did cause a movement; he came towards her and rested a hand on her shoulder. 'She used to laugh at me – because of Mother but I could not help that.'

When he caressed her shoulder he said, 'Of course you couldn't help your mother's possessiveness. I would have thought Bron would have realized that. But then if she was a kid at the time – well, kids don't think sensitively, do they?'

'No, I suppose not. But enough of all this gloom; it's all in the past. Bron will find Jack, she'll forgive Jack and they will live happily ever after. They might even decide to stay over there.'

Nothing. No emotion. 'Perhaps they will,' he said. 'But what I really want . . .' his voice went dark and interesting. 'What I really want is to talk about Marged. Just who are you, Marged?'

'Just an ordinary girl.' She looked up at him, widening her eyes, parting her lips. His head bent and he touched her lips with his own, very gently. His lips were cool and pleasant; it was a kiss but not a passionate one. However, she could wait, she did not want him to think that she was easy.

She could tell he approved of the table setting. His eyes took it all in. He ate well and heartily and was a perfect guest. She watched him all the time beneath her lashes, taking in the smooth skin, the tantalizing dark eyes. She liked dark-eyed men. He looked just a little more Maori than his sister, although Ruthie had a look of him. Job perhaps took after his father and when she mentioned it he smiled and nodded. He was proud of his heritage, he told her. He had been to Scotland too. It was not unlike South Island, he said, but it had been cold.

'How far back was your Scottish family?' she asked.

'Oh, my great-grandmother. Their stories have always been handed down. It was quite a romance. They ran away together. Her family disowned her for marrying a man that they termed a native. But they were very happy and in love. She was a remarkable lady, she did not let the sticks and stones break her bones.'

'She must have been very brave – for that time especially. What was she called?'

'Eliza MacLennan.'

'My father was Welsh,' Marged said. 'So we both have something of the Celt about us.'

'Yes, we do, I never thought about it,' he smiled. When he smiled a small perfect dimple appeared at the side of his cheek. He is what I want, Marged thought. I want to be his Eliza MacLennan.

Later, in her bed, she wondered if it had been a successful evening. The food was delicious and Job was an entertaining guest but Marged was not certain that she had got what she wanted.

Apart from the rather chaste kiss and a repeat before he left, there had been no *real* overtures. He asked her lots of questions, albeit in an easy, laid back way, but had it been interrogation? She sat up, her heart hammering now, irritation robbing her of sleep. Had he used her to find out about Bron? But he had barely asked about Bron, so it could not be that. Her mind started to spin with suspicion. What had he wanted? Not to make love to her – that was so obviously not on the cards. Why had he come? She had been so sure that she had him but now she was overwhelmed with doubt.

She knew he would not be an easy catch but she had not expected that he had a motive for dining with her that was not to do with her!

Insecurity washed over her; she could not sleep and left the bed to pad into the kitchen. She put on the kettle, and then switched it off again, going into the living room to wander around. This was what she wanted – this and Job Tepi – but somehow she was failing. It was Bron; it had to be Bron that was spoiling it for her, just like she spoiled everything for her.

Eventually she went back to bed to sleep fitfully. The doorbell chiming wakened her. Sluggishly she dragged herself from the bed and went to the door.

When she saw who it was she stepped back, putting a

hand up to her throat and then looking out to see if they were being observed.

'What are *you* doing here? You shouldn't be here!'

CHAPTER EIGHT

HE did not want to leave the body on the path. Besides, she was still warm. The outdoors was not something he enjoyed either. There was a small rise to the side of the road, on the other side of it a narrow stream.

He took her by her legs after throwing her knapsack over the knoll. He dragged her; she was heavy for him. When he reached the knoll he was puffing and panting like he had run ten miles. After pausing he rolled her up and then over the knoll. She rolled down right into the stream.

He could hear the sound of larks. It irritated him. Quickly he straightened out her body and pushed her face into the stream. He intended holding down her head but he heard a sound of something different from the larks. It was a high pitched whistle. Looking up, he saw a cluster of sheep coming over the hill, at their heels two brown and black dogs. Somewhere behind them there had to be a shepherd. He could not afford to wait. She was going to die anyway; her face was in the chilling water. The shepherd would not see her.

He bolted, pulling his hood over his head, running down the footpath. He reached the stile and scrambled over it and instead of taking the path she had done to get up here, he went to the right where there looked to be another path. He thought it might lead down to the river. Anyway, it would get him off the hills quicker, he was certain.

One of the dogs broke free from sheep duties; he was young and still reckless. He smelt water and was thirsty, so he headed down to the stream. When he got there he took strong gulps. The water tasted different – meatier than water usually did – and he lapped ferociously. He could hear now the shepherd's angry cry and the sharp sound of the whistle.

Bella, his mother, had left the sheep; she was down beside him giving him a nip at his leg. He yelped and turned to escape but something had alerted her; her ears were up. She sniffed the air and ran upstream.

The shepherd was raining curses on both dogs now, and the sheep were standing in a nervous group, moving to the right and then to the left.

Bella saw the person in the stream; she bounded over, barking ferociously. When she reached the body she took hold of the soft jacket collar, yanking and pulling, just as she would do with a sheep that had fallen face down in water.

Owen Isaf arrived then, bending over the body, turning it over and murmuring in his musical tones to the inert woman. He bent over her, blowing air into her lungs, turning her over when he felt her move; there was little water in her lungs but what was there came up. He saw the mass of blood on the back of her skull; it stained her dark hair crimson.

His son had bought him a mobile phone. He had moaned about it at the time, wondering what he would ever do with such a contraption, but it proved useful now. It was powerful and he got a good reception, even up here. First he tele-

100

phoned Isaf Farm and spoke to his wife. She would get on to the mountain rescue and the police.

'What happened to you, girl?' he murmured gently, not anticipating a reply. He was holding her hand, and he felt the slightest pressure and then her eyelids fluttered open, just for a brief moment. She stared at him and then they closed again.

Ellen Cabins was saying: 'Owen Isaf it was that found you – remember him, Bron? Has Isaf Farm, had that nice looking son, went to Cardiff, he did – done well for himself. Well, he found you, or those dogs did, good dogs those, is it? 'Specially Bella. Pulled your face out of the damn stream, good dog she is.'

Bron smiled a little, enjoying Ellen's musical voice. It was like having Mam back again. She squeezed Ellen's hand gratefully.

She remembered walking the hills and pausing to look up the path to where the gate was. She knew she had been thinking about the wonderful views on the other side but she could not recall what had happened.

'Did I fall?' Her head was hurting as if a thousand and one imps were in there playing with hammers and chisels. 'I can't remember.'

'Fall, my arse,' Ellen said. 'Someone clobbered you, girl – got a bloody lump on your head the size of a grapefruit, Owen Isaf said, and so much blood. Shoved you into the stream too – who would do that to you, girl?'

'I don't understand,' Bron murmured.

'You're not to worry yourself, Bron. Doctor says take it easy for a couple of days. Sent PC Plod on his way, he did, told him to come back Friday. I tell you, it is a good job we still have our cottage hospital otherwise it'd be Bangor for

101

you girl, and no visitors, is it? I wonder what happened to Jack. Lazy sod, where can he be?'

'I wish I knew. But surely no one would . . .'

'Get some funny buggers coming here,' Ellen announced. 'Know we are trusting and don't lock our doors, or used not to. Just come on spec, see you. Probably thought you had money in your backpack.'

'Well, only a couple of ten pound notes, for train fare and my tea in town,' Bron murmured. 'It's a mystery, Ellen.' She raised a hand but even that movement hurt her head.

'Well, don't you worry yourself about it now, Bron. I'll keep the cabin for you, don't worry. Got to look after our own, *cariad*.'

'Bless you, Ellen.'

Bron's eyes closed. Certain she had fallen asleep, Ellen tiptoed out. 'Look after her,' she said to the nurses. 'She's a lovely girl, that one.'

But Bron only dozed lightly; her mind was so troubled. She had imagined she had fallen and now Ellen was saying something else. Who would attack her? She could not believe it was a random attack. There would be no point.

She knew a girl had been raped on the hills a while ago and they had never caught the perpetrator. That had been random and opportunistic but her attack – what was that? There had been no rape – God, there hadn't, surely? She rang the bell and the nurse came in. 'Someone hit me on the head,' she said, 'I can't remember anything.' The nurse came and patted the sheet. 'Don't worry yourself, Bron. Bad as it is, that was all. A blow to the head, nothing else, my love.'

When the nurse left, a voice whispered in her ear and she put a hand to cup her ear as if to drive it away. *It could be Jack*, it whispered. Jack would have so much to benefit from your death. Desperate men do desperate things. No, not Jack. Whatever he had done to her financially he would not harm her. Jack did not have a violent bone in his body. She might not have known her husband as well as she thought but of that she was certain.

When the nurse brought her evening meal, she asked, 'Are you sure there is no one we can call, Bron? No one at home? Doctor says we can phone New Zealand, is it.'

She thought for a moment. She did not want to call Marged. But there was Ruthie. Ruthie could tell them at school what happened. Marged would make a drama out of her crisis but Ruthie would not. Why did I think that, she questioned herself, about Marged? Yet instinctively she was remembering things about Marged that she had forgotten. 'She's sly,' her mam had said. 'I would not trust her far as I could throw her. I am sorry for her being stuck with her mother all the time, but that doesn't mean I have to like the girl. You watch her, Bron, I don't like the way she sometimes looks at you.'

'Mam, there you go, that dark Celtic soul of yours, seeing things that aren't there. She's OK. A bit too quiet for me but she isn't a bad kid.'

'No, love, I did not mean she was bad. Just sly, there is a difference. Just watch her.'

No, Marged would not be the one to call but Ruthie, steadfast and honest. But there was her brother. A rush of guilt overwhelmed her. Job had warned her – but surely the attack was random? People had not followed her here. She was being paranoid.

'Nurse, I'd like to call New Zealand. It will have to be in the morning about eight, if that would be all right with the doctor? Otherwise we are looking at late tonight.'

'Doesn't matter, Bron. They'll charge you for the call anyway.'

Bron smiled. 'No problem, then.'

Ruthie answered the phone after only a couple of rings. Bron felt a rush of warmth, and tears swam into her eyes. The people at the hospital and in the village had been so kind, bringing her flowers and fruit, but she felt a connection to Ruthie that was overwhelming. She had not realized how much she had come to really like the woman.

'How are you?' Ruthie asked.

'I'm in a bit of a pickle, Ruthie.'

'A what? In trouble, do you mean? What? Do you want, money? What is it, Bron?' Ruthie sounded full of anxiety.

'No not money, you see . . .'

Ruthie had been adamant. 'Get over here now, Job,' she said, 'and no messing about.'

He came quickly, swinging his pick-up on to the drive and running into the house. He imagined a catastrophe – his nephew seriously ill, his brother-in-law at death's door and at best the house collapsed around his elder sister.

'What is it?' he asked, looking around for signs of the disaster.

'Are you keeping something from me, Job?'

'What do you mean?'

'About Jack and, more importantly, about the way he has treated Bron. Do you know more than you have ever told me? I want to know, Job. I am not playing here.'

'Look, Ruthie, I know what you know. I don't know where he is. Is this what this is about, bloody Jack? That waster? You dragged me from my business because of him?'

Ruthie eyed him, looking for secrets. Her brother was a successful businessman. He had made a lot of money from small beginnings. She thought he was on the level but how did she know what he got up to in Auckland? She knew he was not a criminal but she thought there were things about him that she would rather not know.

'Not because of Jack, or maybe Jack is in there somewhere. It's because of Bron.'

'Bron?'

Now he looked worried and that pleased her. 'Bron was in Wales, out walking in the hills. She got attacked. She's OK now but it was pretty serious. If a farmer hadn't found her, well . . .' Ruthie's shrug was significant.

'That bastard!'

'What bastard?'

'Jack. He has to be behind it. He tricked her out there.' He made a fist of his right hand, slamming it into his left, leaving no doubt as to whom he was imagining he was hitting.

'She doesn't know who it was but she doesn't think it was Jack. He didn't turn up where they should have met. He still hasn't turned up.'

'Or so she thinks. She told me she was going back to where they used to live. She didn't tell me she was going to Wales. She lied to me. You know, I thought she was lying but then I thought, not Bron, she is too honest.'

'Never mind what she said, now is all that's important. Do you really imagine that Jack would do that? I had no time for him but violence – and to Bron. It doesn't ring a bell with me.'

'He's in deep trouble,' Job said. 'And with some nasty individuals. I think he is desperate enough to do anything. With Bron out of the way he gets the house and whatever money she has.'

'If he went to Bron with his problems she would have

helped him out. I know that and he must have known it too.'

'You think?'

'She doesn't want *her* to know.'

'I'm sorry?'

Ruthie nodded her head. 'You know who I mean, your dining companion of a couple of nights ago. Blondie.'

'Why wouldn't she want Marged to know? She's her cousin. I don't know what you have against Marged.'

'Don't you? I suppose not, seeing as you are always sniffing around her like she's ice cream.'

'Ruthie.' He took hold of his sister and gave her a hug. 'Don't be so . . . impossible.'

'I'm not being impossible, but you are backing the wrong mare there. Anyway, that's beside the point. You are not to tell her. I am not even supposed to tell you but I wanted to see if you knew anything. I just have to let them know at school.'

'I won't tell Marged if Bron doesn't want, but I can't see the harm. Just where is Bron exactly?'

'I'm not to tell anyone that either.' Ruthie turned away. 'You can go now seeing as you can't help.'

'She'd be better off back here. I can go and fetch her.'

'No, she doesn't want you to know. I told you that, Job. She will know that I betrayed her and she won't like it. She was adamant.'

Job shoved his hands into his trouser pockets. He seemed to be staring into space but his mind had to have been ticking over, for he said to Ruthie, 'Phone her and ask her if you can tell me. Explain that she can get back here quicker if she has an escort.'

'You'd do that? Go over there and bring her back?'

'Yes, I would.'

Ruthie weighed her brother. 'I thought you had your eye on Blondie,' she murmured. 'But it's Bron, isn't it?'

'It's neither,' he denied adamantly. 'Bron is a good friend, that's all, and the other intrigues me a little. I can't make her out. It's just curiosity.'

'Well, just you remember where curiosity led that cat.'

'I don't know,' Bron said. 'They won't sign me off to fly yet anyway. I have to wait a couple of weeks. Seems concussion can come on later. I think it's all nonsense, and I feel great now.'

'No, you don't,' Ruthie said intuitively. 'Your head must feel really sore. Skulls don't heal overnight, you know. Even if they sign you off it's a long way to come on your own. He really would want to help.'

'Does he?' Bron tried to keep accusation out of her voice. 'You've told him, Ruthie, haven't you?'

There was a long silence until Ruthie admitted the truth. 'I'm sorry. I thought he might know something. Anyway, Bron, I don't know what you have against him. You might have your reasons, I know that. He is a dark horse but he's my brother and I love him but I know he has another life. Bron, he would never harm you. He has a great respect for you and he was genuinely worried.'

'I don't know,' Bron murmured once more. Doubt was fading but why should he want to do that? Come to the other side of the world just to fetch her home. It did not make for any kind of sense. Not unless he knew things about what had happened to her.

'I used to think we were good friends, Ruthie, but he let me down. I'm sorry but he really did. He knew things and he never told me.'

'What kind of things?'

Bron sighed into the telephone. 'He knew about Jack and the things that were going on in Auckland.'

'I see. And had he told you, what then? Was it his place to dob in your husband? Would you have believed him? Surely you would have had doubts. You knew Jack, you hardly know Job. Who are you going to believe? It's a lot to ask a man to do, come between man and wife. That is dicey territory, Bron, can't you see that?'

Bron was honest enough to admit that perhaps she would not have believed him. After all, it had come as a shock to realize how deceitful Jack had been. She had never thought that her husband would do such things.

No, if she was being truly honest with herself, then she doubted she would have believed Job Tepi if he had come with tales. Ruthie was right about that. If Jack had denied it all she would have taken him at his word. In the end she asked Ruthie to let her think about it overnight.

Tomorrow morning she would leave the cottage hospital and go back to the cabin. She was nervous about it. No, more than nervous – she was frightened. Instinct told her it was not a random attack, such things did not happen, not here. Someone wanted to hurt her. The only thing of which she was certain was that it was *not* Jack.

Next morning she knew what she would do. She would let Job Tepi come. During the long night she had tossed in her small hospital bed. There was an unpleasant lump in the centre of her chest: it was fear. She recognized it. She was no heroine. Someone had wanted her dead and if they found out they had failed, what was to say they would not come back again?

There was a sturdy lock on the cabin door but Ellen, anticipating how Bron would feel, had been out and bought a padlock and chain.

'Bit over the top,' the big woman said, 'but better safe than sorry if there is a nutter out there, *cariad*.'

'Thank you, Ellen, I really appreciate that. I have a friend coming to join me,' she said. 'His name is Job Tepi and I think he will be here by Saturday. Is it OK if he stays here?'

'Of course, not a problem, love. It's your cabin – you can have anyone you want to stay, just so long as I know for fire rules, is it?'

'Great.' Bron felt herself blush and knew that she needed to exonerate herself. 'Er, he isn't that kind of friend. I mean, he will have the sofa bed.'

' 'Course he will.' Ellen smiled, and then proceeded to give Bron a big hug. 'Bron, I've known you too many years. I know you were looking forward to Jack coming. I didn't think for one moment you would be two-timing him.'

No, Bron thought, but he has probably two-timed me, many times. 'He might come – Jack, I mean. The only thing is . . .' She hesitated. Of course she trusted Ellen but Ellen liked to gossip. 'I don't know when,' she finished lamely. She had been going to say what had only just been revealed to her by the police, but Ellen need not know about that. It would only complicate things. She had better to keep it to herself and perhaps, after seeing how he made her feel when he arrived, Job Tepi.

Her sleep that night was less disturbed than she had thought it would be. She did not take the tranquilizers that the doctor had prescribed; she knew she needed to be alert should something happen. Perhaps it was Ellen's double lock, but she drifted off to sleep and did not waken until turned seven.

The day turned warm and sunny; the mountains beckoned but she was too afraid. Instead she slipped a swimsuit under her summer dress, took up a towel and drove down to the beach. There would be other people there and she would be safe in the crowd.

It was not too busy. The beach was long and sandy, stretching for ten miles, protected at the back by huge dunes, and there were a few families and couples enjoying the early summer weather. The sea was not as warm as she liked but after walking out gingerly, she eventually rolled into a wave and once she started to swim she found it not too bad. The beach shelved very gently and she maintained her depth without fear of getting caught too far out.

Later, having dried off, she wandered to the pub and sat in the garden. She ordered lunch, enjoying watching small children playing on the swings in the garden to the side of the pub.

The landlord kept the garden himself and it was always immaculate; the lawn smooth and green and clipped as neatly as a bowling lawn. The rockery was full of flowers and there was a monkey puzzle tree by the hedge, its dark green branches twisted like dozens of dark green, feathery creatures.

The landlord came and chatted to her, commiserating with her over what had happened, declaring that it was terrible that such a thing could happen here. A couple of local farmers who knew her stopped as well, expressing their concern. She knew most people who lived in the village: she had come here first as a little girl with her parents and every year for at least a long weekend before they left for New Zealand. It was home from home. Yet for all the warmth and friendliness, she felt a sudden panic rising inside her. She made her excuses and bolted for her car.

She needed to be inside the cabin, the locks on the door. The panic attack was real and frightening. Even though the doctor had said she would experience these feelings, she had not really believed him. She was tough and strong . . . yet when she finally reached the cabin and bolted and locked the door, she burst into tears.

Someone wanted to harm her and she could not understand why. Although it was warm, she climbed into the bed, dragging the duvet over her head. She was shivering violently, her sobs loud and horrible even to her. Where was her past life? Her lovely, contented life? But perhaps that was part of it, she had been too content and she had not seen Jack spiralling into a terrible world.

Ellen looked at the man. She had never seen anyone quite like him before. He was – and the word drifted into her mind – exotic. Handsome, yes, and the denim jacket and matching jeans and white T-shirt, were perfect on his frame. Ordinary clothes, to be sure, seen around the area often enough, but on *him* the simple clothing had a whole new meaning. His long black sleek hair, held back with a thong of sorts, emphasized the broad cheekbones, the fine curve of his nose. Bet he knows he's gorgeous, Ellen thought, finally dragging her eyes off him.

'So you're Mr Tepi,' she said. 'Bron said to expect you. I'll come with you. I am not sure if she has gone out.'

'Lead on,' he said with a devastating smile, swinging his flight bag on his shoulder. He did not have a suitcase. The taxi driver that dropped him deposited no bags on the forecourt.

Bron's car was parked on the hard-standing at the side

of the cabin. The curtains were drawn across the windows. It was lovely and sunny and that seemed a strange thing to do in the middle of the afternoon. Ellen tapped on the door, hesitated and, hearing no reply or sound of movement, called out.

'Bron, it's Ellen, I have Mr Tepi with me.' Ellen knocked again, only louder this time.

There was a flutter of sound, bare feet padding across the wooden floor. Ellen heard the padlock being undone, and then the key turning in the lock. She shot a look at Tepi, he had raised an eyebrow. The door opened part way. 'Oh,' she whispered, and then pulled it fully open on seeing who was there.

Job stepped back a little. Bron looked terrible. Dark shadows circled her eyes and she looked as if she were on some kind of debilitating drug. He saw she had lost weight and that she had lost that sparkle that was always part of her essence.

'Well then, caught you napping, did we?' Ellen said brightly. She looked back over her shoulder at Tepi. 'I'll leave you to it,' she said. 'If you want anything just give me a shout.'

Discreetly Ellen left, not even looking behind her although the temptation to give Tepi another look was difficult to resist.

'You'd better come in, Job,' Bron said. She seemed to need to hold on to the lintel as she parted the door even wider. He wanted to help her, take hold of her and steady her but he didn't do so. She was fragile and vulnerable and he was not certain how she would take his touching her.

It was relief that made Bron sway a little, not relief that it was Tepi but that someone would be with her. Being alone had started to terrify her. Only weeks ago it had been a luxury she had relished, especially since Marged had moved in with her, but now it seemed a burdensome, terrifying thing.

Tepi put down his bag and then just stood looking at her. He opened his mouth to say something, changed his mind and instead asked how she was.

She was honest but then that was Bron. A straight-talking woman, he had always liked that about her. 'Terrible.' She pushed her hair back from her face. 'Mentally more than physically, I feel so . . . I mean, I get these panic attacks.'

'That's natural, Bron.'

'Let me make you some tea.'

'I can do it. You sit down before you fall down.'

'God, do I look that bad?'

'Pretty much.'

She took his advice and went and sat in the armchair. It took him moments and no instructions from her to put on the kettle, find cups and a teapot. He did everything quietly and efficiently, without fuss or noise.

'I am grateful to you for coming over,' she admitted.

He poured boiling water over the teabags in the pot, found a tray and came and set the things out on the small table by her side.

'There,' he said, pouring the tea and putting in sugar but no milk. 'Just how you like it, and I'm glad to help, Bron. It helps me with my guilt.'

She looked at him sharply. 'What guilt?'

'My guilt at not telling you what Jack was up to originally.'

'I wouldn't have listened,' she admitted. 'I would have believed Jack no matter what evidence you had. After all, I thought I knew him very well.' She was quiet for a moment.

113

He took the chair opposite her and helped himself to tea. He thought it better to let her talk it all out of herself. 'Why does someone want to hurt me?'

'I don't know, Bron. But I sure as hell am going to find out – *somehow.*'

They sat in silence as the minutes ticked by. After a while she started to talk about mundane matters, telling him where he could sleep, asking him what he liked to eat. Was he sure he could spare the time? There was another week before she would have the all-clear to travel.

'Don't worry, I'm OK. This is nice, I like it. I want to take you out. I want you to show me the area. I've never been to Wales before.'

'Well,' she smiled for the first time, a gentle rather sad smile. 'I love it myself. Job, there's a lot I want to talk about, but not now. I've been so frightened and the feeling's leaving me now that you're here. I feel peaceful. Does that sound mad?'

'Not mad at all. In fact, it's rather flattering.'

'I didn't say it to flatter you. But I feel as if a heavy stone has been rolled away. I can breathe again. I felt so rotten, Job, so out of control. When you came I was hiding under the duvet. I've been doing that a lot – it's quite irrational and not like me.'

'Not like the *real* you, Bron, but you have had a terrifying experience and things like that can make you do irrational things. How about I take this newly found you out to eat tonight? There is somewhere to eat out, isn't there?'

'Oh yes, a few good places, actually.'

'You'll let me do that, then? Take you out?'

'Yes Job, and thank you. I'd really like that.'

He gave her a penetrating stare. It was not the kind of thing she would say. She had always been polite but not obsequious. Her lids were lowered over her eyes; she could not meet his eyes. This was definitely not the Bron he knew. He decided he would not say anything, after all, it would only make her more self-conscious if he brought her attention to how she had changed.

Her nerves were all of a flutter. The moment she walked into the pub she felt as if someone were watching her. Hesitating for a moment, she cast her eyes around the room, saw a darkened corner and headed there. There was a settle against the back wall but she chose the armed chair that allowed her to have her back to the room. Job said nothing but pulled himself, with a little difficulty, on to the settle. She thought of his long legs. 'I'm sorry, I can't face the room,' she murmured.

'No worries,' he said with a warm smile. 'This is nice.' He studied the room, looking at the brasses on the walls. The lighting was subtle, and there was an air of the old world about the place that he liked.

'This used to be a convalescent home,' she went on, 'for the miners in the south. The area used to be fairly dry, I mean hardly any alcohol sold. At one time there was no pub for about ten miles but things have changed a lot. They even have Sunday openings now. They made a good job of the conversion.' Her words were spoken quickly, as if she could not wait to get them out of her mouth. Every little movement betrayed how nervous she was.

'You remember when it was a convalescent home?'

'Oh yes, I always loved the house. I liked the long windows. They shone so brightly in the evening when the sun was setting, it always seemed a happy place. I don't know if it was but it seemed that way. It's made a lovely pub. The food is all home cooked.'

It was the landlady that came to see what they wanted. She knew Bron and chatted to her for a moment or two and Bron introduced Job. She could see that Job was causing quite a flutter because one of the girls that worked in the kitchen came and brought their wine. Of course, Job seemed exotic here whereas in New Zealand he was merely a good looking Maori.

Bron was right: the food was delicious. He filled her glass with wine. They had walked down to the pub, he had suggested it. It was only a mile and along a country lane that had little traffic. Oddly she had seemed all right until she had come into the pub, then he saw her physically tremble.

'You mustn't let them win, Bron,' he counselled. 'You're stronger than that.'

Her eyes met his; there was a spark of anger there that he was glad to see. Her spirit was only submerged.

'I'm not going to. But I can't help this feeling that comes over me. I know the pills the doctor gave me would help but I don't want to feel woolly. I think I would rather have the panic attacks than that.'

'That's up to you but maybe you would have been better trying the pills. Now I'm here you don't need pills. Nothing is going to happen to you while I'm here, Bron. You must believe that.'

'Thank you. Job, there's something I have to tell you.' She reached a hand across the table. It was the first time she had touched him since he had arrived. When they had walked down to the pub they had walked side by side but she had been independent of him, keeping a sliver of distance between them. Her hand looked small, resting on his, and so pale against his brown skin. He twisted his hand, until he held hers firmly.

116

'The police came to see me.'

'I should hope they did.'

'No, I mean a few days ago. I had told them my story – oh, not the whole saga. I mean, I didn't tell them about Jack and his troubles. I just told them that he had e-mailed me to meet him here. They came back to see me because they had checked. Job, Jack hasn't re-entered the country. At least, he hasn't under his own name.'

Job straightened, his eyes narrowing. 'It figures,' he muttered.

'Look, Job. I think something is wrong. Jack wouldn't come under a false name. I just know he would not have the *guts* to do that. I know he pulled the wool over my eyes pretty thoroughly, and I would never have thought he could do that, but he would not do something criminal. He wouldn't know how to go about it.'

'Gamblers make odd friends,' Job murmured, at the same time tending to agree with her. Jack was weak and stupid but Job did not think he was sharp enough to do something like that. Besides, the very people who could have provided him with the means to enter Great Britain undetected were the very people who were after him for the money he owed them.

'He wanted you out of New Zealand, which is why it's important for you to get back there.'

'He can't do anything, Job. He won't know where to find the deeds to the house and I haven't any money.'

Job wanted to say he would need only to turn up if you were found dead and everything would be his. However, in spite of what he thought about Jack Mellor, he did not think he would have had the necessary touch of evil to murder his wife. As to someone else doing it for him, who would he know, apart from those pursuing him, who would

117

do such a thing? And Jack hadn't the money to make it worthwhile anyway. Yet if they thought there was money in it. . . .

Who else would want Bron dead? Sure, Jack was being pressured by some individuals who were not adverse to permanently removing anyone – but why remove Bron? She could lead them to Jack unwittingly. Besides, she part-owned the house. They would see that as being money and money was their god.

Would Jack really give her up to them? He might have thought it unlikely but there was something else he knew. He looked across at Bron. To tell or not to tell. Tough choice. If he told her it would scare her to death. If he didn't tell her, he left himself open again to charges of being deceitful.

He knew that Jack was not the kind to plot murder. But would he really care if Bron was murdered? Had he gone that far that this would be seen as an end to his problems and to hell with this girl he had married and once, presumably, loved? No, he thought something was missing, although he had no idea what it was. He opted for not saying anything, and yet at the same time hated himself, even though his motives were pure, for not telling her.

Could it be that it was a random attack? He looked at Bron. Aware of his perusal of her, she dropped her eyes. The blow to the head had really knocked some of the stuffing out of her. Now and again she showed a trace of the real her but she was not the woman she had been. He hated them, whoever they were, for doing that to her.

She had been walking alone and had crossed the path of a nut looking for someone to hurt. It wasn't anything to do with Jack or his stupid behaviour. It was a coincidence. Yet the thought persisted: it had been an e-mail purportedly from Jack that had brought her here. Whoever had sent that e-mail knew what kind of place this was. Had they also known her routine when she was here? That she always walked that path through the mountains?

'What do the police think about it?'

'They don't say directly but I get the impression they think it was a random attack.'

He was still holding her hand tightly; he lessoned his grip, smoothing a finger over the delicate bones at her wrist. She seemed to dare herself to meet his eyes. 'Then let us say that was what it was,' Job said. 'And when I get you home, you just get on with your life.'

She wanted to say it would never be that simple. After all, she had the panic attacks and they would not leave her for some time. Then there was the mystery of Jack getting her here in the first place. Jack had not been in Great Britain but someone had; someone who knew that they both loved this place very much. That it was special to them.

Had they made Jack tell them? Had they wanted the house to get their money? It was all too farcical. She did not move in those kinds of worlds, so how could she know what people would do? However, she expressed none of these doubts to Job. He wanted her to believe that it was a random attack and she wanted to believe that too.

'You're making me feel a lot better, you know, Job. I'm glad you came. I'm sorry I didn't want to involve you at first, really sorry. Thank goodness Ruthie made me see sense. She's a wise woman, your sister.'

'She's that all right. Now tell me something else. What do you think you are going to do about Marged?'

She laughed. It tinkled out of her, warming him, making him see that she was still in there – *somewhere*. 'Goodness, Job, am I that obvious?'

CHAPTER NINE

BRON awoke. There was a noise and it was more than the wind whispering through the trees. A thin pencil of light showed under her door. She listened. There was a murmur. As quiet as possible, she slid from the bed. Her heart was beating madly but she could not stop herself from crossing the room. She part opened the door. It was Job, with his back to her, and he was talking into a Blackberry.

He was speaking too low for her to catch his words but she coughed delicately and stepped fully into the room. He turned, held up a hand and with a forefinger beckoned her.

She looked at her watch: it was only 1 a.m. She thought she had been asleep for hours and was surprised that it had been less than an hour. He ended the conversation, putting down the phone, but he did it leisurely and not as if he had anything to hide. He said, 'Ruthie. I thought I'd let her know how things were.'

She nodded. Of course, it would be afternoon in New Zealand. 'I'm sorry if I disturbed you,' he said. 'I haven't got into a sleep pattern yet. I was having some coffee, do you want some?'

'If you want to sleep you're better staying off the coffee,' she said. 'But I wouldn't mind a cup of hot milk.'

She went to the fridge and took out the milk, setting the pan on the stove and then, suddenly conscious of what she was wearing, she froze to the spot. 'Watch the milk, please,' she said to Job, before scurrying back to her room and slipping a robe over her thin silk nightdress.

The milk had boiled and he had put it in the cup by the time she returned. He thankfully made no comment about her exit.

'Apparently Marged's been around asking where I am,' he said.

'Really? And does she have the right to make those kinds of enquiries?'

'What do you mean?'

'Well, is there something between you two? I rather had the impression she wouldn't be adverse if you were interested.'

Clang! She heard the sound in her head, what a stupid thing to say. It sounded spiteful and jealous and she was neither of these . . . or was she? Job was not her personal property and he was single as was Marged. It was nothing to do with her.

'I'm not having an affair with Marged,' he said, but only after leaving her words hanging in the air for some time.

'I didn't mean that exactly. I mean, I thought you might be dating or something.'

'That's an old-fashioned concept.' Now he was teasing her. She could hear it in his voice.

'This is going nowhere.'

'That's the same as Marged and me. Marged has no reason to ask questions about my whereabouts. Ruthie accused me of the same thing. I wonder what it is about me that make people think I can't resist women.'

'I think you give that impression. You can be very charm-

ing when you want to be. Anyway, what did you tell Ruthie
to tell her?'

'That it's none of her business but she'd done that
already. Marged works for me and I have been friendly
with her but no more friendly than I have been with you.
You never put tags on me, Bron. I've never known you ask
me where I've been when I've been out of town.'

'I'm sorry, Job, I shouldn't be judging you. I had no right
to ask you anything. I shouldn't say but I will be honest.
You see, I have a problem with Marged.'

'You do?' His eyes were twinkling across at her.

'I don't like her very much. I'm ashamed to say it but I
can't help it. Something about her rubs me up the wrong
way. Even when we were kids we never got on.'

'There's nothing to be ashamed of, Bron. I have relations
I can't stand. We talked about it before, remember? I said
it's true that God gives you your relations but thank God
he lets you choose your friends.'

Bron went and sat on the settee. Surprising her again,
Job came and sat beside her. For a moment or two she did
nothing but sip her milk and then, as if someone had
opened a gate in her mind, she told him about Marged.
About when they were younger and the way she tried to be
friends with her cousin. It had never happened. They did at
best *suffer* one another.

'I blame her mother, she was so possessive. Marged was
never allowed to do anything herself. I think that's why she
is as she is. I think this must be the first time she has ever
been left alone to think for herself.'

'Don't fret over it, it isn't your fault.'

Her hair had fallen over her cheeks, and very gently Job
reached out and tucked the dark silken strands behind her
ears. She turned, a question in her eyes. 'Ssh,' he

murmured. 'Everything is going to be just fine.'

Before she realized his intention, he had cupped her lips with his own, very gently, his lips cool and soft, his light kiss causing a feather of delight to move over her. Down in her belly it danced, travelling along her spine, even to the very tips of her fingers. She parted her lips a little, letting her hands slide up over the smooth cashmere of the sweater he wore.

His body felt hard, his shoulders broad and strong. Her lips, unused for so long, responded and cajoled and when he deepened the kiss she was ready, opening herself up to him, letting her breasts crush against his chest, delighted as his hands at her back drew her closer. One hand curled at the nape of her neck, brushing aside her hair, a thumb manipulating the warm flesh.

When his mouth released hers, he went to cup the tiny lobe of her ear in his mouth, she moaned in pleasure, unable to control the little delighted gasps as his hands travelled over her.

She had been left cold and lonely for so long, her arms empty, her body aching for fulfilment, longing to feel the warmth of someone close to her, now she was a flower, opening up to the sun. Her head bent back, his lips travelled the length of her throat, moving inexorably to her eager lips and once there he thrust deep inside her mouth with his tongue, finding her own tongue waiting and eager to mix and tease and play. . . .

Her hands sought his flesh, beneath the sweater, marvelling at the feel of muscled, firm skin, her fingers teased his nipples, feeling him tense and shudder.

He moved from teasing her mouth, his breath coming in short deep gasps. 'Bron, this is the wrong time . . .'

'No, you're wrong – it is so the right time.' In case he

escaped, she wound herself around him, loosening the robe she had earlier run to cover herself with, her mouth seeking his, feeling immediately his response. She knew he wanted to stop on a matter of principle – she was the vulnerable woman. That was what he thought but she needed so much more, now, tonight – she needed to feel wanted, she wanted to be a woman again. 'I want you, Job,' she confessed.

'Sweetheart,' he murmured against her lips, pulling her down into the comforting folds of the settee, sliding his hand down the neckline of her nightdress, cupping and caressing her breast, exposing its pouting centre and covering it with his mouth. Bron gasped at the pleasure, thrusting her limbs against his own, feeling the warm gush of liquid pool at her thighs.

His searching fingers found her moist centre, moaned her name. As he caressed her gently he allowed himself to wonder for a dizzy moment where the contained and self-sufficient woman had gone. Had he dreamed her and this passionate creature spilling herself on his fingers was she real one?

'Bron, this is insane,' he said.

'Yes,' she murmured, 'I know it is but it is wonderful too, Job . . .'

'I'm sorry,' she murmured. Job lay on his back, his hair loose from its tie, fanned out across the pillow, dark and thick and rich. There was sheen across his brown-skinned chest; she saw the rise and fall as he took a deep breath.

'There is nothing to be sorry about,' he said at last, turning to slide his arm around her. Not daring to meet his frank gaze, she lowered her lashes over her eyes. Part of her wanted to run from the bed, throw herself into the shower and wash the shame out of her, the other part wanted to say, I want *more*. I want to do it again and again – now in this bed that we somehow stumbled on to.

'I don't know what happened.'

'Well, if you don't know, then I am the man to tell you.' His voice had that teasing quality that she knew so well. Everything was so wrong. They had been friends. For a short time she had suspected him of all kinds of things but in the end had turned to him in trust again. Now what had she done? Ruined their friendship by allowing sex to rear its ugly head!

'I don't mean that, I mean . . . I don't know what I mean.'

'You know what your trouble is, Bronwen, you analyze things far too much.'

'Agreed,' she honestly admitted.

'Instead of just enjoying life. What happened? You're a woman . . .' He reached up, brushing back her hair. 'Look at me, Bronwen,' he commanded. She opened her eyes and met his dark-eyed stare. Just for a moment, there was something so mysterious about his eyes – hypnotic, certainly, but something hidden perhaps. If the eyes were the windows of the soul, then his soul was buried deep.

'I'm a man and there has been an awful lot of sparks for a long time.'

She denied that hotly. There never had been any sparks, or was she lying to herself?

'Have it your way,' he said. 'Perhaps it was just me. You were strictly out of bounds anyway. I don't play around with married women.'

That was nice to hear. It warmed her heart. 'It has just complicated things,' she said.

'There are no complications, only the ones that you put up. If you want me to walk away, I will. If you want to see . . .' He shrugged.

'See?'

'Where life takes us.'

Her hand went out, not really in protest but just a movement. It met his naked flesh, her palm felt singed, and
down inside her she felt a swelling, frissons of delight tripping across her stomach, an aching yearning at her
breasts. She almost gasped with the intensity of it; just
touching him made her want him. Frightened suddenly by
such unusual passion, she looked up at him, her eyes, unbe-
known to her, giving away her feelings. Her lips parted
involuntarily, the sudden rush of blood through her body
turning them crimson.

'Oh, Bronwen,' he murmured, putting out a finger and
moving it across the pouting fullness of her lower lip. Her
tongue slid out of her mouth to run across the finger in a
provocative gesture. 'Who are you really?' he muttered and
then, giving in to the feverish demands of his own body, he
pushed her back against the pillows, his mouth capturing
hers. Her arms and legs held him fast, her body moving
sensuously against his own, demanding the essential fulfilment that she knew that union with him would bring. It
was so wrong and yet it was all she wanted – to be part of
him, part of this enigmatic man who had always intrigued
her. She had to admit that, had to be truthful with herself,
especially now.

Next day they explored the countryside together. Job drove
and she gave him directions. She took him to favourite
spots, to see magical castles, to travel high mountain roads
and to park and walk and look at the glorious landscape.

It was different. Their friendship was still there –
because they had shared that, they knew how to talk to one

another without shyness – but there was so much more. He would take her hand, or pull her to him in a deep hug. There were brief kisses. He draped an arm around her shoulder as they walked, took hold of her hand in a restaurant where they stopped for lunch. Their shared intimacy had really changed things.

She said, as he drove them back to the cabin, 'It was over with Jack, even before he left. I just did not want to admit it. I think I was afraid of being alone. I suppose that's a terrible basis for a relationship. It could be that I drove Jack to seek other pleasures.'

'I don't want you blaming yourself for Jack's inadequacies.' He spoke to her very firmly. 'None of it was your fault. If he felt you drawing away he should have spoken up. If you were making him unhappy he should have said so. In a relationship you have to have total honesty otherwise it's not worth having that relationship. And I knew that your marriage was ending, Bron,' he said.

'You did?'

He sighed. 'To me you did not seem troubled by his absence. You were getting on with your life. You were independent and happy. Am I wrong?'

'No, I just didn't realize I was so obvious.'

'You weren't to anyone else, you just were to me because I . . .' He hesitated. 'I was making a study of you.'

'You were?' It gave her pleasure to hear it; it was not frightening at all.

'You fascinated me.'

She stopped herself saying delightedly, 'I *did*?' although she wanted to.

'I had no idea.'

'Well, I was not going to tell you. I don't prey on other men's wives, as I said before and you know, Bron, I have some standards.'

'It's nice that you do,' she said, and she meant it. What would she have done had he come on to her? She had not been as honest as he; she had not admitted that he attracted her, just as she attracted him. That was why she was always pleased to see him when she went out on the boat, or when she met him in town. If she was honest then he fascinated her too. However, she felt that was too much information for now.

'And as for Jack, I really wanted to dob him in but . . .' He shrugged, uncomfortable with what he had to say. 'I was not sure that if I did so I was doing it for the right reasons.'

'What do you mean?'

'Was I telling you because I wanted to cause trouble, then be there to pick up the pieces, or did I want to tell you because I did not like the way he was treating you? See how difficult it was for me?'

'Yes, I think I do. Anyway, I doubt I would have believed you. I really trusted Jack. Says a lot for my common sense, doesn't it?'

'No, it says a lot for your loyalty and you can't buy that. I only wish you could. You have to see the doctor tomorrow, Bron, so if he says it is OK to travel, when do you want to leave?'

Leave this idyll, back to the real world. She almost laughed. New Zealand was paradise – hardly a grind going back there. But it was what was there. The reality of their lives and of course the presence of Marged at her house.

'I . . . well, as soon as we can, I suppose.'

'Yes, that's good. I'll be happier when you're home. You will be safe there and all this will seem like a bad dream.'

'Will it? You really think my attacker was random?'

'Nothing else makes any sense.'

She leaned towards him, resting her head on his shoulder. He took one arm off the wheel and slid it around her, pulling the car into the side of the road and then sliding towards her to find her lips parted and moist and eager for his kisses.

'Everything is going to be fine,' he murmured against her ear, his tongue tracing the fine contours.

She sighed and moved restlessly. 'Job, you have to know what that does to me.'

'Sure I do, and you have to know what it does to me too.'

'Let's go back,' she said breathlessly.

'We can never go back, sweetheart, only forwards.'

Marged was furious. That stuck-up bitch Ruthie had told her, in no uncertain terms, that it was none of her business where Job Tepi was. As if she was nothing and no one.

'But we're good friends.'

'Job has a lot of *friends*,' Ruthie said. 'I would not read too much into it!'

She wandered around the house feeling restless. The comfort she had gained from having the lovely house to herself was fast eroding.

The job at the hotel was not as exciting as she had first thought, and she had made no friends, not that she had made any effort. One girl had invited her to Scottish country dancing and Marged had given her a withering glance before turning away. Did she look like someone that would enjoy that? She was not Bron, for goodness' sake, who would probably revel in such nonsense. No, she needed to do something exciting.

The prospect of a trip to Auckland seemed tempting; perhaps that was where Job had gone. If she went she might meet him – as ridiculous as it sounded it was not an impossible prospect. It wasn't as if Auckland was that big. Besides, she had an idea where his apartment was. Jack had told her the general area, so if she was in the same vicinity there was a possibility that she would run into him. However, there was a problem with Auckland. Someone else was back there now, someone she thought it better not to see just yet.

Marged sighed. Life was not working out as she had planned and wasn't that just typical of her. The fates were always conspiring against her.

The highly polished floorboards caught her eye. The sun was coming in through the open shutters and the wood looked warm and inviting and so perfect. Muttering under her breath she went into Bron's room. Did the woman have a shoe fetish? She had lots of shoes, some quite expensive stilettos. Marged had never been able to wear anything like that. Her mother had told her that she would topple over in really high heels and break her ankles. She chose the red patent leather pair that she had worn for Job Tepi. Tart's shoes if ever she saw them.

Back in the lounge she went to the long French glass windows, the ones that let out on to the veranda. Kneeling, she took the stiletto and scraped it along the wood. The bright sunlight illuminated the mark. She gouged another one and then in a flurry of frustration just ran the heel of the shoe across the surface. Made breathless by the action, she at last cast the shoe aside and just knelt, looking with satisfaction at the damage she had caused. The pleasure she gained was orgiastic in its intensity.

When she felt calm, she took up the shoes and went out to the trash. She dumped the shoes in the bin. The men would come for the garbage tomorrow. Throwing away something of Bron's gave her almost as much satisfaction as damaging the floor had.

She remembered the past, how she had stolen a teddy bear that Bron had loved. She had smuggled it away and set fire to it. Bron had been miserable for weeks because her stupid bear had gone missing, almost as if it were a real thing and not a stuffed toy.

There were other things she had taken too: small things, pieces of clothing, stuff that her cousin really liked. Of course she had never been found out. Bron's mother had consoled her daughter, telling her she must have given the items away for a jumble sale, taking the blame, never telling her daughter that it was Bron who was careless with her things. That's what Marged's mother would have done – she would have blamed her for everything, and she frequently did. When things went wrong it had to have been Marged's fault.

Bron always had everything: a kind and loving mother and father, lovely toys, smart clothes, a chance to go to university, marriage to Jack who, to Marged, had seemed a real dreamboat, only she had not realized what a pain Jack really was. Now Bron had this lovely house, a well-paid job, success and ... Marged felt her heart beating rapidly again. Had she had Job Tepi too?

'I'm sick of being alone here,' she complained to herself. 'I will go to Auckland. I need company. I need . . .' With a sly little smile and almost in a whisper, as if afraid someone would hear her: '*Sex*. And he is very good at sex. It's worth the risk.'

She had her bag packed and had she been quicker she would have missed Ruthie. *Ruthie!* The very sight of the woman infuriated Marged. What did she want, she wondered, glancing back at the floor. The scratches were

131

quite significant and she did not want Ruthie to see them. Ruthie had come in after knocking on the kitchen door and was making her way from there to the sitting room. Marged rushed to meet her, blocking her at the kitchen doorway.

'Oh, Ruthie, I wondered who it was. I thought it was Bron ... sorry, I'm just about to go out.' She was determined not to tell the woman where she was going, although she had left word at the hotel that she would not be in for three days because she had urgent business in Auckland.

'That's all right,' Ruthie said. 'I won't keep you. Bron was on the phone. She's booked her flight home and she will ... Marged?'

She saw the girl pale. The blood ran from her pink lips and a hand went out to the architrave, clasping it as if she was going to faint. 'What did you say?'

'Bron's coming home. Whatever is the matter with you?'

'I thought she was—' Marged cut the words off and searched around for something to say but found her usually fertile mind empty.

Ruthie's eyes narrowed. 'Yes, what did you think?' Ruthie persisted.

'That she and Jack were having some kind of reunion, like a second honeymoon.' The words spilled out of her at last. 'I thought they had gone to France or somewhere romantic, being reconciled.'

'Are they *reconciled*?' Ruthie asked.

'I thought so. I thought that was why I didn't hear anything. Anyway, if you knew they weren't, wouldn't *you* have told me?'

'Not really, Marged. It's not my business to tell *you* anything. Only just now, I spoke to Bron and she said she would be home on Tuesday. She wanted you to know.'

'I won't be here,' Marged said. 'I've been called away urgently on business.'

'You're going back to England?' Marged read the pleasure in the question. The woman could barely hide her dislike.

'No, not to England. You can tell Bron that I should be back by the weekend. Is Jack coming with her?'

Ruthie looked at the other girl and saw that the colour had come back into her cheeks and her lips. Why had she seemed so shocked to hear that Bron was coming back? What information did she have that would cause her to act like that? Second honeymoon, stuff and nonsense. Ruthie tried to analyze with her practical mind what would cause such a reaction. Nothing came to mind, but the girl had been upset. Definitely. She had not imagined that.

'She didn't say,' Ruthie said at last. And that was not a lie because she had not mentioned anyone, not even her brother. The message was simple: *Just tell Marged I will be home Tuesday, will you, Ruthie. That way if I am home late she won't be surprised if she is in bed.* Thoughtful, Ruthie had thought, but then that was Bron.

'You'll have to excuse me, Ruthie, I have to get off.'

'Sure, I'll buy some fresh food for when she gets back. Don't you worry yourself about details like that.'

'Don't worry, I won't.' Marged could not stop the words and anyway she realized trying to butter up Ruthie was never going to work, so why waste her time trying.

After she had gone, Marged went back into the house. She went to Bron's room and then to her wardrobe. She had seen a nice cream satin blouse; it would just about fit her and would go with her black pants. She dragged it from its hanger and went and put it in her suitcase.

The doorbell rang. It would be the taxi to take her to the

car hire office. Picking up her suitcase, she walked out, throwing the hanger on to the bed.

'You are tired,' Job murmured. 'Don't lie to me.' He reached over, smoothing a forefinger over the dark shadows beneath her eyes.

'Why would I be tired?' She smiled up into his dark, dark eyes. 'I had three whole days dashing around Los Angeles, then I was tired. But three days relaxing on a south sea island, come on!'

He had arranged it all, had taken her open ticket and talked to the airlines. He had made their journey so easy with these interesting stopovers.

'But you have had a lot to get over,' Job insisted. 'That's why, when we land, I'm going to take you to my apartment. We can drive up north tomorrow.'

'Oh, really, and just where is your apartment?'

'In Auckland.'

Watching her closely, he saw her pale, observed the way her hand trembled as she brought it up to her face. Guilt? Did she feel guilty about their relationship because of Jack?

'I'm a little apprehensive,' she admitted.

'Why would you be that?'

Why indeed, she wondered. After all, they had hardly had a platonic relationship on their journey home – certainly not! But Auckland. What if Jack turned up and discovered them? So what! her lively mind answered her. He had sent her on a wild goose chase for some nefarious purpose – oh, not to have her nearly murdered, she was convinced Jack would not do that, but to somehow get her out of New Zealand. There was nothing between her and Jack any more but between her and Job there was . . .

what? She didn't know and had no intention of asking him. Suffice to know that what she had going with Job at the moment was delicious and unlike anything she had had in her life before. Not just the love-making either and that was . . . the word *fantastic* came to mind. She had had no idea what she had been missing in life and also what she did not *know* about! It had come as quite a shock to realize that she had never had a *complete* orgasm, that previously she had merely teetered on the edge. No wonder when she and Job had first made love that her first words were, '*What was that?*' But there was even more than that glorious realization, there was conversation and laughter and warmth. She had real fun with Job in and out of the bedroom.

I'm not going to care about Jack. Just like he ceased to care about me a long time ago, if he ever truly did *really* care. Considering the years of their marriage, she had come to realize that he had certainly not cared enough.

'All right, your apartment it is. I'm in no hurry to get home.' The thought of Marged and what she and Job would not be able to do because she was around came into her mind. A depressing thought. She had better enjoy what time they had together. Who knew what the future would hold.

'Now that is sensible. I don't feel like driving north anyway. How about we have dinner out and—'

'How about we have dinner in,' she murmured.

'That's fine by me, just so long as dinner is in not because you don't want to be seen with me.'

'Job Tepi – you can't be serious!'

'No, not entirely serious. But you might be thinking about Jack.'

'Bugger Jack,' she said, and then she laughed.

135

'My thoughts entirely.'

Job's apartment was by the harbour, a penthouse with a spectacular view of the bridge and the boats in the bay, all the way across to Devonport on the other side. There was a balcony, a large lounge, ultra-modern kitchen and three bedrooms each with its own bathroom, as well as a smaller room that he called the den. Everything was very neat and tidy but he said he had a lady who came and 'did' for him, otherwise it would be a complete tip. He was not good at doing everything for himself; he had no interest in it.

'I used to when I was a kid,' he said. He smiled warmly. 'Ruthie used to make me and if I didn't she would really come down on me. Now I don't need to and don't see why I should. What do you think?'

'It's me you're talking to. I hate housework. I am the least domesticated woman in the world, but I can cook so that is my saving grace.'

'I know you can cook.' He came to her, drawing her into his arms. 'I've eaten dinner at your house and even in the cabin you managed to produce a lovely dinner for a last meal there. Don't ever put yourself down to me, Bron.'

'I wasn't, I was being honest. I do housework because I have to, not because I want to. I think that would go for a lot of women too. How come we always get landed with the housework role?' She laughed into his eyes, then snuggled into him, enjoying the feel of him next to her, the smell of him, and the hard angles of his body, so different from her own slender curves. 'I think I'll take a shower. I need it after that flight. How come flying always makes you feel so grubby?'

'It is grubby, even in first class,' he murmured. 'All that recirculated air.'

'Ah yes, that was another thing. How come you got an upgrade?'

'Baby, I'm marvellous,' he said. 'Now what do you want to eat? Say it and I'll call out for it.'

'Something from the mystic east I think.'

'Chinese? Thai?'

'Perfect. Either one will be fine.'

It was wonderful; they ate by the huge plate-glass window, looking out at the twinkling lights below at the harbour and on the far side of the bay. The food – Chinese – was delicious, the wine from the Marlborough region perfectly chilled.

Bron realized she was happy, but felt odd that she should be happy in such circumstances. After all, she did not know where Jack was, what he would do next and she had been almost killed, yet she was happy, happier than she had ever been. *Ever?* Surely that was an exaggeration. Well, she had had happier days but she realized they were days shared with her parents. This kind of warm feeling of contentment and satisfaction was rare, she admitted honestly to herself.

'What are you thinking? You have that dreamy look in your eyes.'

'Do I?'

'Yes, it is incredibly sexy, do you know that?'

'Goodness, no, and I don't believe you. I was thinking that I feel . . .' She hesitated. How could she tell him the truth of how she felt? He might take it on himself to bolt. Yet she was not one for prevarication. 'That I feel content.'

He looked at her appraisingly, not smiling, not frowning. 'I'm glad, Bron, because I want you to feel like that every day.'

'Wow, I can't promise that.'

'Neither can I but I would like it.'

He poured more wine into her glass. Then, standing, took away their dishes. He went and put them in the dishwasher and when he came back he stood behind her, resting his hands on her shoulders, kneading the flesh very gently, his lips brushed her hair. 'I love the way your hair smells. It's like newly mown grass. I like everything about you, Bron.'

She leaned back against him. 'Don't stop, I love it!' She was not sure whether she meant his massaging of her shoulders or the words he said. His voice was deep and warm too, she liked that about him, always had. And that slight New Zealand accent. The way words like *check* sounded like *chick*, she founded it endearing somehow.

He bent his head, smoothing her hair from her neck, his tongue circling the pale flesh at her nape. She moaned a little, feeling the little darts of pleasure erupt at all her secret places, her limbs melting, her thighs parting. His hands slid over her shoulders, down her chest, resting and cupping her breasts, a slight moan erupting from his throat as he felt them braless, and eagerly his fingers reached for the zipper on her top, sliding it down, parting the material so he could tease the already hard nipples. 'Bron,' he murmured, 'do you know what you do to me?'

She could not answer, could not find the breath to form words. He drew her up from the chair, still keeping her back to him, urging her back into an embrace as his hands now eased down the sweatpants, his hands playing with her belly, fingers stretching to the curl of hair at her mount. Her arms reached up behind her, going into his hair, around his neck, her body arched fully against his, aware of the growing tension of his maleness, hard against the contours of her bottom. His fingers played her now, teasing the velvety smoothness of her essence. She cried out her need, demanding from him that ultimate fulfilment. Slowly, as if he had all the time in the world, he turned her around, crushing her to him, lifting her into his arms and carrying her to the bedroom. Once there he laid her very gently on the silken sheets, gazing down at her.

'Bronwen,' he said. Her name choked out of him as he came to her, holding her against him. She reached up to him, winding herself around him, and in husky whispers implored him to take her now at this perfect moment.

Later, with the dark night all around them, he whispered her name once more.

'What is it?' She felt a little shy; she always did later because she did not recognize the woman she was in their intimate moments. That wanton passionate creature he made her.

He twisted a lock of her hair around his finger. 'Nothing,' he said at length, 'just Bronwen.'

His car was in the underground car park. She slid beside him; he turned and kissed her before starting the engine. Slowly he went up the ramp, waving to the attendant and then pausing to let pedestrians pass. Dreamily, blissfully tired, Bron gave the pedestrians scant attention and then one person caught her eye. She started up; the man scurried across the ramp and jogged on. Pressing her face to the side window, she stared after his retreating back. Job turned left, the way the man had gone. The car passed him still jogging on the pavement. She cranked her head around to stare back at him. She *knew* him from somewhere, she was certain she did. The man jogged around a corner. Job, concentrating on driving, barely noticed her concern. She started to say something and then firmly closed her mouth, pressing her lips together. She was being ridiculous; the man was a complete stranger to her. He just looked like someone she thought she knew – but who was that someone? By the time she remembered they had crossed the bridge and were leaving the city traffic behind. Realization of who the man resembled made her smile a little. Fancy remembering him after all these years!

'OK?' Job asked the question, giving her a quick look.

'I'm fine, more than fine in fact. And you?'

'Oh, sweetheart, need you ask?' He was smiling, almost to himself. She felt herself flush a little. Was he thinking about something that had happened that morning? 'You know what I like about you?' he asked.

'No,' she answered, the word showing her apprehension.

'Apart from all the things I knew *before*,' he emphasized the before that left her no doubt as to what he referred. 'Your essential niceness, your honesty and your warmth, those things I knew about, but it's you, the way you look, so prim and proper, your hair always nice, clothes stylish but neat.'

'Oh, like a schoolmarm, you mean.'

'Well, a bit, but you're very stylish. Preppy I think is a word to describe your style. I suppose classy is what they'd say in England.'

'Like now, wearing jeans and a striped top.'

'Well, not all the time but in the main when I used to see you out and about, not on the boat or down at the marina, obviously not, but generally. Anyway, I like it because no one would guess that you are incredibly sexy. I like it that no one would guess. Call me a male chauvinist pig if you want, but I do like that.'

'You're making me blush.'

'I know and I like that as well.'

Bron thought about it for a whole five minutes. She almost heard the seconds ticking away as she debated whether to say anything. What the hell, she thought, I have to be honest.

'It's you,' she said, 'it's how you treat me, it's what you do. I never thought . . .' No she could not say that. It would be a betrayal of Jack and it was unnecessary to do that, no matter what he had done to her. It was probably not even his fault.

Job was generous so let it go, and he said no more on the subject, instead asking if they should stop for coffee.

'Whatever suits you,' she said, glad he had changed the subject.

'OK, we'll press on if you are not bothered. I have to be somewhere this afternoon.'

Not wanting to ask where, she in reply merely reached across and squeezed his thigh.

'I'm happy if you're happy.'

'You're not worried about Marged, are you?'

'A little,' she admitted.

'Well, don't be. I never gave her any reason to think anything would come of our acquaintance. To tell you the truth . . .' He hesitated. 'I couldn't care less who knows about us. How about you?'

Knows about us? That sounded so promising. *Us!* It warmed her and made her sing inside.

'I'm not ashamed, Job of anything. I am happy. It doesn't matter to me who knows.'

'She was in a big hurry to go somewhere. Auckland I think,' Ruthie said.

'Well perhaps it's as well,' Bron said.

'I'll make you coffee.' Ruthie bustled into the kitchen. Job pulled Bron to him.

'I have to go. It's as well she's away, gives us time to be . . . together.'

'Together?'

'Later, I'm going to come and take you to dinner and then . . .'

'You want to stay here?'

'Sure, if you want me to.'

'It will be strange,' she admitted.

'If you want to go somewhere else, we can do that.'

Bron looked up at him. He seemed concerned, worried even. 'No, no, I don't. I want this – whatever it is.'

'Whatever it is?' He bent and kissed her nose lightly. 'You are so funny, Bron. I'll be back for seven.'

He left via the kitchen. She heard him saying something to Ruthie and his sister laughed.

Ruthie came out with a tray containing two mugs and the coffee pot. There was a jug of cream and a bowl of sugar, together with some cakes that she must have brought.

After putting the tray down, Ruthie gave what Bron could only describe as an old-fashioned look, head to one side. 'You look better than I thought you would,' Ruthie announced at last, then seeing the dark flush invade her friend's cheeks, she turned away and busied herself with the coffee.

'I'm not going to lie or hide things from you, Ruthie, only Job and I . . .'

Ruthie held up her hands. 'You don't have to tell me anything.'

'Well, he might be around more often and . . .'

Ruthie let out a little squeal. 'Oh heavens above, I never saw that coming! You mean you and my brother? Yippee, it's a dream come true! I've prayed for some woman to come along and tame him and I knew it should be you!' Ruthie came over to Bron and gave her a big hug. 'I'm so happy!'

'Well, it's early days and—'

142

'I don't care. I am just so pleased I could burst out in boils and squeeze myself to death!'

Bron laughed gaily. 'Oh, Ruthie, you are so hilarious, come and let me give you another hug.'

They talked for some while. Ruthie was concerned about how Bron was feeling, how she felt about what had happened to her. Her hopes and fears. Then, after going quiet and looking just a little uncomfortable, Ruthie said, 'She was wearing your clothes. I recognized stuff.'

'Well,' Bron shrugged a little, trying not to show her irritation at this news. 'She hasn't many clothes.'

'She must have, she was always coming back with carrier bags, and it wasn't food in those bags.'

'I know you don't like her, Ruthie, but I have to try to get along with her to a certain extent, her being family. I don't think she will be too happy about Job and I, so I will have to face that bridge when I come to it. If taking my clothes helps her accept it, she can have the lot.'

'I don't like her. It's irrational but something about her bends my antenna and I don't like it, Bron. I don't want to be this way about her. I've tried but she gives me the creeps. I can't trust her.'

'She is a strange girl, always was, but she isn't a bad person, Ruthie. She had a terrible life. I make excuses for her, I know, but she really had. I can never feel . . .' Bron hesitated trying to find the words. 'I guess I can never feel close to her, but I have to try.'

'I can appreciate that. If you say she's not bad then I will go along with it, but she did want to get her claws into Job.'

'Well, who could blame her?' Realizing what she said, Bron put a hand up to her mouth as if to push the words back in. Ruthie beamed.

'It's OK, I won't give away your secrets, but you have to

know, Bron, you can trust him. He's honest . . . at least I think he is.' Ruthie winked.

'I think I've realized that. I've realized a lot of things since I got that bump on the head. For a long time I made compromises, and I don't want to do that any more.'

'I should say not. Live your life to the full. You deserve it, Bron, you're a good person.'

'Oh, I'm not that!'

'Yes, you are, don't put yourself down. You have a kind way with you. I've seen you with the children at your school – they adore you. You have such a way with you.'

'Well . . . I do like them but, oh, Ruthie, it wasn't what I wanted to do. I didn't have this great vocation to be a teacher, you know.'

'But you are so good at it.'

'Well, that's me, I suppose, I have to win. Competitive, I suppose you'd call it. Whatever,' she shrugged. 'I don't like failure, so I did a good job. But it wasn't what I wanted. I'm going to turn my life around.'

'Really? And how?'

'I'm not sure but I want something different. I did think about doing something with boats. Do you think I'm mad?'

'Not at all. You should talk to Job about that, he could offer you some good advice.'

'I will – sometime but not yet.'

'You can do anything you want to do, Bron. You've got guts and determination. You'll get there, wherever that is, if you really want to.'

She moved her shoulders as if embarrassed. 'I don't know about that. But I will certainly try.'

'Well, you do what is best for yourself. You know . . .' Ruthie hesitated. 'Changing the subject back to Marged, she looked a bit odd when I said you were coming home, almost as if she did not expect you to. Another thing, she seemed convinced that you and Jack were reconciled and that you had gone to, I think she said France, on a kind of second honeymoon. Why would she think something like that?'

'I can't imagine. Unless it was wishful thinking on her part. Maybe she hoped Jack and I would get together again. Perhaps she thought she'd have more chance with Job with me out of the way.'

Ruthie mulled over it for a few moments. 'No, Bron, it was more than that. It made me feel uneasy. You watch her, Bron. I don't trust her one inch.'

'My mother used to say that,' Bron admitted. 'I really miss my mam. She would know the right thing to do about everything.'

'About Job? Only you can decide what you want to do about that.'

'Oh, not Job. I think my mam would have fallen for him too . . .' Bron's hand flew up to cover her mouth again. She was just giving out too much information regarding Job Tepi. Ruthie smiled.

'Maybe he does have a certain appeal for the ladies but he isn't one to mess around, you have to believe that, Bron. Job is not the kind of guy to go in for one-night stands. Never has been.'

Bron smiled. 'As far as you know.'

Ruthie spread her hands in a defeated kind of way. 'Well, yes, as far as I know.'

After Ruthie left, Bron emptied her suitcase and shoved stuff in the washing machine. Her bedroom was as she left it, apart from a clothes hanger on the bed, so obviously Marged had not been sleeping in her bed. She checked her wardrobe but did not notice any missing clothes. Perhaps the girl had borrowed a sweater or a pair of pants. It did not matter, she realized, they were only clothes.

Later she thought she would air the house. It was not cold and the sun was shining, so she opened windows and went to open the French windows that let out on to the veranda. Beams of sunlight streamed in. Turning from the doors her eye caught the gleaming floorboards. Deep white scratches were illuminated in the sunbeams that danced into the room.

She bent down on her knee; it looked like the boards were ice and then someone had been doing a very fast spin on skates. She ran her fingers into the ridges and wondered how it could have happened. It wasn't as if someone had walked across the floor on stilettos, the scratches were too random for that. Had Marged been dancing on this spot in high heels? Even if she had been tap dancing, the scratches would surely not look like a child's scribbled drawing? Besides, she had told Marged that people did not wear shoes in the house in New Zealand, that it was polite to remove your shoes at the door, and take slippers.

'Damn,' she muttered. It did not even look as if the damage would be repairable without taking out a large section of the floor. If she ever sold the house, as she might have to one day, then it would have to be repaired. There was no use in putting a rug over the marks; it would not be fair to any prospective buyer to do that.

Sinking back on her haunches, she suddenly realized the impact of what she had thought of doing – selling the house, the house she loved. But she would need to pay off Jack when he surfaced. There was no way she could pay him without selling her lovely home.

'I can't make these decisions now,' she said out loud. 'Too much has happened to me and I am rushing ahead with ideas and schemes that haven't been thought out or discussed.'

Depression came to her, even though she counselled herself with the thought that it was only a scratched floor. But that was not the root of the depression, the root lay in the mystery of the damage. Had Marged done it in a fit of pique. But why would she be having a hissy fit? She had not known that Job had gone to the UK. Even more sinister was the thought that it was not Marged. Someone other than Marged had been in the house and done the damage. But why? Was it as a warning? As proof that they could get into her house whenever they wanted? Bron shivered, even sitting in the warm sunlight, she felt cold and folded her arms around her. Something was very wrong and she was not able to see the full picture. That was frightening.

It went a little cooler as the sun fled the sky. She went around closing windows and doors but did not bother lighting the wood-burning stove. It was not cold, she felt chilled because of something inside her, nothing to do with the climate.

By six the laundry was done and put away but she was still in the jeans and sweatshirt she had worn all day. Hurriedly she took a quick shower, washed her hair and padded back into the bedroom. Flicking through the clothes in her wardrobe she found a plain black woollen dress that she had always liked. Taking it down, she lay it across the bed before towelling herself dry and slipping into a cream silk bra and panties. When she saw her reflection she thought the dress looked rather severe and went to her jewellery box. The single strand of pearls that had belonged to her mother seemed to smile up at her. She chose to wear them and the matching earrings. Her hair would almost be dry by seven so she did not bother with the hairdrier, just paused long enough to add a little blusher and lipstick, feeling that she looked wan without.

After collecting a pair of black high-heeled shoes, she went out into the sitting room, trying not to look at the scratched floor, but it seemed to call to her and she had to go and look at it again.

'Damn,' she muttered not for the first time, before determinedly turning away in order to light the lamps.

She felt restless and she did not want to feel this way. Happy was what she wanted. Her eye caught the black shoes. No, not black – she would add a touch of red. Red always cheered her. Going back to the wardrobe, she rummaged through, looking for her high-heeled red patent stilettos. Odd, they were not there. She looked again and then again and realized she was getting in a panic. It was her teens again, things missing, lost or . . . she sat back. *Marged*. She had to have taken the shoes. Bron knew she had not lost them. Ruthie had said she had seen her wearing Bron's clothes. Flicking quickly through the wardrobe, she saw other things were missing: a satin blouse, a bright yellow jacket. Angry now, she slammed shut the wardrobe door. It was just one more thing she would have to deal with. Marged would have to be told and it was not something she looked forward to.

Going back into the sitting room, she mulled on the reality. It would be a wrench to sell the colonial house but she knew she would have to. She could not afford to give Jack his share without doing so, and she definitely was not up to arguing with him about it. No matter what he had done to her, how he had taken most of her money, and the proceeds of the sale of the boat, she knew she would give him his share of the house.

She wanted a quick divorce; there was going to be no

dragging it through the courts. The sooner he was permanently out of her life the happier she would be.

The bell rang out. It was a quarter to seven. She went to the door and opened it, not expecting Job at all. Seeing him gave her a feeling of pure delight. After her afternoon of misery it was wonderful to feel all that depression fly away. Get a grip, girl, she counselled herself, because this is not going to be for ever. Job is not a for ever kind of guy! But what the hell, her optimistic side told her, just enjoy what is being offered.

'You could have just come in,' she said.

'Oh no, that wouldn't be right.'

'Why ever not?'

He looked at her for a long moment. 'I don't know, I guess I could have. It did not seem right.'

'Would you like a key or am I rushing ahead?'

'When you are living alone, then I will have a key,' he said, 'but until then I'm going to be formal, OK?'

'I forgot about that and as always you're right.'

'No, I am not always right, Bron. You look gorgeous, do you know that?'

'No, I don't know that but you can keep telling me. Anyway, come in. Do you have time for a drink?'

'I have time for anything you want,' he murmured, causing a slow, intense fluttering at her stomach. 'However, a coke would be great. I'm driving you somewhere special tonight.'

'That sounds intriguing.'

'You get a glass of wine, there's no hurry to get off.'

It was good, she was happy, emptying ice cubes into a glass, tipping in a good measure of coke and then taking it to him. He had gone to sit on the settee, his legs crossed looking like he belonged. Job never appeared uncomfortable. He was happy with himself, she thought, that was how she wanted to be too. Happy with who she was and not always aspiring to be what someone thought she should be.

After she had poured herself a glass of wine and gone and sat beside him on the settee she told him about the floor. 'I know it's silly but it just feels so odd.'

He said nothing but sprang up and strode across to where she said the floor was damaged. He went down on his knee, running fingers over the damaged surface. 'This is bad, have you a stiletto?' he asked.

She got up and took one of the shoes she had left by the door for wearing that night. It was a stiletto. She gave it to him and he looked up at her. 'I'm just going to go in the middle of this scratch. The whole thing will have to be taken out so it won't matter.'

He rubbed the heel in the centre then sat back and looked at it. She knelt beside him; the scratch was identical to the others. 'There, that's how it was done, with a stiletto.'

'How did you guess that?'

'Easy, a girl did it to my car once. I swear I was innocent of any crime against her,' he said.

'I wouldn't doubt it. Dump her, did you?'

'No, I never took her out but she thought I should, that kind of thing.'

'Irresistible man eh?'

'Some would say that but it's not important, what is important is that someone did this and I think I can guess who.'

'Who?'

'Come on! You aren't thinking Jack, are you? Or those thugs he owes money to? Believe me something like this is a woman's thing. The thugs would have wrecked the room;

they don't know how to do gentle damage.'

'You don't mean Marged, do you?' But she knew it was right.

'I mean Marged, that same Marged who asked me to dinner and wore that pearl necklace.'

Her hand went up to the necklace, the pearls warm how against her throat. She asked him how he could be sure. 'Those are real pearls, they have a certain glow about them, and they're quiet old, aren't they?'

'Grandmother's,' she said. 'Then my mam's and now mine.'

'They are the same, I'd bet my last dollar on it.'

'Well, just because she wore my pearls it does not mean she damaged my floor. I mean, what could she get out of that?'

'What could the girl get out of damaging my car? She just annoyed me and cost me a lot of money to put it right. It's a way of getting at you. Marged doesn't like you; she thinks you were cruel to her when you were younger.'

Bronwen blushed and lowered her eyes for a moment. 'I was a bit. She was strange even then and I didn't help. I used to resent having to entertain her because we had nothing in common. And I mean nothing. But she had a rotten life and I should have been kinder to her. But you can't put an old head on young shoulders, can you?'

'No you can't, and you've been good to her since she came, so what is she playing at?'

Bronwen did not say but she thought she knew. It was simple. Job Tepi. Just as Marged had envied Bronwen her clothes when they were younger – and her friends and books and toys – she now envied her friendship with Job Tepi. There could be no other explanation. And if she envied her that friendship, just how more potent would that envy be when she realized she now had Job Tepi as her lover. She decided not to mention the missing shoes, or the clothes the girl had borrowed, or taken. These were material things and did not matter, but the floor, that was pure spite.

'You know what I think?' Job interrupted her thoughts. 'I think we should forget all about Marged. I think we should go out as planned and enjoy ourselves. I'm going to take you out to have the best fish and chips in the world.'

'Hey now, that is something you are going to have to prove, matey!'

'I bet you ten dollars I am right.'

'You're on.'

It was one of those strange evenings. It was not as cold as it should have been for the time of year, and it was a perfectly clear night. He drove them north and pulled into the car park of a restaurant. The restaurant was built on stilts over the ocean. Moored up were lots of boats, swaying gently in the ripple of breeze.

'Mangonui fish and chips, best in the world, I tell you.'

He did not lie. She had to concede they were the best ever. She gave him his ten dollars and he took it, pushing it in the top pocket of his jacket. She liked that. Unlike Jack, she liked to pay her debts and she could see he saw that about her.

'That was the best I have ever had,' she said. 'How do they do that?'

He shrugged. 'Have no idea, they just do. Look, some mates are having an evening of entertainment. Are you up for it Bron, or will it be too much for you?'

She linked her arm in his. 'Job, I am up for anything that you are!'

'Well now . . .' But he led her to the car and then when

they were settled drove north again.

Eventually he drove the car off the main drag and down a rutted lane. When he pulled up she could hear the sound of music and laughter. 'This sounds like fun,' she murmured.

They walked down the lane a little way; she took off her shoes and felt soft sand between the ruts. There was a beach house at the end of the lane and then the beach and the soft, swishing swell of the Pacific.

There were a lot of people, both Maori and settlers, and they were all gathered inside and outside of the large rambling house. There was the smell of barbecued food and the sound of joyous laughter. All ages were there, kids and the elderly and people her age.

They were greeted with warmth and it was only a moment before she realized she really was being welcomed. The friendly greetings were not just for Job.

He took her hand and they went and danced on the shore with other people. The lanterns of light were being blown by the wind and casting myriad colours along the shore-line. The enormous sky was littered with stars and the moon looked huge in the dark sky. Beneath her feet the sand felt soft, like mountains of chalk drifting through her toes. It was crazy, something so different and yet so wonderful.

'I don't think I have ever been so happy.' The words slipped out, but perhaps they were lost in the music and laughter for Job said nothing. He maintained his hold on her but nothing more.

Later they went and gathered around the huge camp fire someone had lit down the beach. There was singing now and people had brought musical instruments.

The singing was glorious, it filled her heart and brought

back so many memories of her mam and Wales and the times they had enjoyed musical parties where people entertained themselves. It was a time she had thought she had lost, and yet she had come to the other side of the world and found it flourishing.

They were whispering about leaving, it being turned midnight, when an elderly man, obviously a relation of Job from their likeness, asked Bron to sing.

'Everyone has to try,' he said with a laugh.

'You mean I have to sing and I didn't have my supper?' she laughed back, having no intention of refusing. She was half Welsh and the Welsh, like the Maori people, loved to sing. Her voice she knew was reasonable, which they could not be aware of.

'Of course,' the older man said. Some of the others protested, calling that it was not fair to put their guest on the spot. A young woman nearby had a guitar; Bron asked if she could borrow it.

After tuning it slightly, she strummed a note and then decided what she would sing. They were a good audience, giving quiet respect. She could hear her voice being echoed back to her in the silence of the night. Her heart felt big inside her, she felt at home and at peace and this feeling of love and friendship ensured the sincerity of her voice.

The applause was loud and appreciative, She felt a momentary shyness and knew she was blushing slightly as she handed back the guitar.

'I knew you could sing,' the old man said. 'I could tell that about you.'

'Well, thank you for that,' she said, smiling.

He leaned towards her, saying so quietly that no one but Bron could hear: 'Let your burdens go, begin to enjoy your life. You deserve to be happy.'

Her eyes widened at the perception of the old man, and there was a terrifying second when her eyes, filled up with tears but she managed to do battle and send them away.

He was right, of course.

Job slid an arm around her waist. 'I didn't know you could sing so beautifully,' he murmured. 'You want to go home now?'

'Yes. Well, I don't really but I think we should. It's late and it's a long drive.'

'I know just what you mean. OK honey, let's say goodbye and get home.'

There was a hammering, it wasn't in her head. She turned in the huge bed. Someone was in her bed . . . She half opened her eyes and through a chink of light seeping in from the curtains, she saw Job's bronzed shoulder. She sighed contentedly and moved closer to him, sliding an arm around his firm, hard flesh. She could not have been asleep hours. It was late when they arrived back and then there had been . . . She smiled, happy with her thoughts.

The hammering was there again. 'Holy—' Job bit on whatever that last word was to be. 'Someone is at the flaming door.'

He went to struggle out of the tangle of bedding. 'No, let me,' she whispered urgently, not ready yet to expose their relationship to the whole town.

Sliding out of bed, she reached for her robe, fastening it as she sped through the house to the front door.

'Coming!' she yelled, as the hammering sounded again. She flung back the door, then when she saw who was there, she stepped back, a hand automatically going to her mouth. 'Oh, sorry – I . . .'

It was two policemen. One was in uniform, the other had

155

the look of a cop although in plain clothes.

'Mrs Mellor, you are Mrs Mellor?'

'Yes, is this about the attack?' The policemen exchanged glances with one another then looked back at her. Obviously they were taking in her tumbled hair, her tightly tied robe, the way her hand had pulled the top part tightly together and stayed there clutching it, as if expecting it to fly open any moment.

'We do need to talk to you, Mrs Mellor. May we come in?'

'Of course,' she stepped back. 'Do come this way.'

Too late her eyes saw the state of the sitting room. There was a trail of clothing leading to the bedroom door.

'Let's go in here,' she said, leading them towards the small den off the main living area.

'Sorry to disturb you,' the one in plain clothes said with a broad hint of sarcasm.

'You're not disturbing me. You just woke me up, that's all,' she answered tartly. She was embarrassed but she was not going to let them see that.

'You said something about an attack, ma'am?' the younger, uniformed cop asked.

'Yes, it happened in Wales . . .' She went on to explain. She heard water running and looked nervously to the doorway, then back to the police again. Why was she so jumpy? Maybe it was because it seemed so compromising, the clothing and everything, her straight from her bed.

'Some time ago you reported your husband missing, ma'am,' the younger one spoke again.

'Yes. But he e-mailed. I just said . . . I just told you that's why I went to Wales supposedly to meet him but he didn't turn up. A friend checked the e-mail, it had generated from the UK.'

'Ma'am, when did you last see your husband?'

She could not think. She remembered he had taken Marged back to Auckland in the summer after Burns Night – January, as long ago as that.

She shook her head, more to compose her thoughts. 'Is something wrong with Jack?' she asked at last, wondering why they were asking these questions.

'Just answer the question, ma'am,'

'No, you answer the question the lady asked you.' They turned. Job was standing in the doorway. Well more he draped the doorway, Bron thought. Very quietly he had to have sneaked out of the bedroom and grabbed his trousers and shirt for he was wearing these now. She noticed however that he was shoe and sockless, and that his hair had not been caught up in its usual tie.

'Mr Tepi.' It was the plain clothes man who spoke.

'Cartwright,' Job said coolly, sauntering into the room to come and stand by the side of Bron. He casually slipped an arm around Bron's shoulder. It felt right somehow, the hand pressing into her lightly but giving her confidence and strength.

'Now, why are you asking these questions of Mrs Mellor?'

'Because . . .'

'I'll do the talking, Constable,' Cartwright snapped. 'It seems that Mr Mellor has been found.'

'Found? What do you mean found?' Bron clutched her robe even more tightly.

'Mr Mellor – and we have ascertained, albeit with difficulty that it was Mr Mellor – was caught up in fishing nets. Apparently he had drowned.'

'Oh my God.' Bron swayed. Job's arms were holding her even more tightly, otherwise she thought she would have slid to the floor.

'You crass idiot,' Job said.

'Are you addressing me, sir?' Cartwright said.

'Who else? Come and sit down, Bron, here.' He led her to the chair by the desk, slowly helping her lower herself on to it.

'He'd been in the water some time.' Oblivious to what Job had said, Cartwright went on, calmly describing the circumstances of Jack's being found as if it were nothing momentous at all. When he finished there was silence for a while and then he spoke again. 'Only thing is, Mrs Mellor, your husband was dead when he went into the water. The pathologist is absolutely certain of that.'

Bron gazed up at him. Job was at her side, squeezing her shoulder hard now. 'I don't understand, Detective.'

'Easy to understand, Mrs Mellor. I am afraid your husband was murdered.'

When would it all end? It was a selfish thought but Bronwen could not help thinking it. She paced the house, going from room to room, her hands clasped around her waist. What had happened to the order in her life? Things like this did not happen to people like her. She led a normal, rather dull life, she was a teacher, and she was living in a country where murder was not at the top of the agenda. Her husband was – had been – a lawyer, not a criminal lawyer but one that dealt with property and probate, nothing that brought him into danger. The boring end of law, that's what he always used to say.

Although Jack had got himself in a mess with gambling, murder should not have been on the cards. It made less and less sense. Why murder Jack over owed money? After all, that would draw attention to his creditors and would make the recovery of any debts nigh impossible. That was not the way it worked unless they thought ... remove *him* and then come after *her*!

Job had gone with the plain clothes policeman. He would go to Auckland to see Jack's remains. In spite of their saying they had evidence that it was Jack, perhaps there was a possibility that it wasn't him.

'I don't want you to do this,' he had said sternly, ignoring the raised eyebrows of both policemen. 'You've been through too much. And you. . .' He turned around to face the policeman again. 'You should have known that Mrs Mellor had been attacked in the UK. My God, they checked with the police over here.'

'I didn't know,' Cartwright said. 'And maybe it was just coincidence.'

'Yeah, maybe it was.' Job was sarcastic.

And she had let him go. It was true she did not think she could face seeing Jack like that. It was cowardly, she admitted it to herself and had told Job, but he was adamant.

She wasn't a coward, far from it, he said, but she had been through far too much. This was a step too far.

Ruthie came over bearing a pot of soup and some rolls. 'You have to have a little something; you look like you're going to keel over, girl.'

She took a little, breaking off a roll and dipping it into the creamy liquid. 'What happened, Ruthie, to my life? To Jack? To us?'

'Nothing of your making, Bron.'

Bron looked up, her eyes awash with unshed tears. 'I didn't love him any more, you know, only I just kept living the lie. Maybe it was that lack of love that drove him to do the things he did?'

'I never knew you had stopped loving him and neither did anyone else. Don't knock yourself out, Bron. He stopped loving you too. And I think before you even realized it. If he loved you he could never have done the things he did. He would have levelled with you and tried to save what you had. That's how it is supposed to work when you love someone, when you are married and in trouble. You go to your partner. You don't go behind their back and steal their money.'

A cold shiver erupted over her body; she clasped the table, feeling weak and momentarily dizzy. Taking a deep breath, it was a moment before she could even say the words that had caused the disruption. 'This is the second murder in our family.'

She slept deeply. The moment her head touched the pillow she thought, I will not sleep, I can't sleep until Job gets back. However, that was the last thing she remembered. She suspected when she woke that Ruthie had put something in the soup, but then realized the thought was unworthy of her. Ruthie would never do something so irresponsible.

Guilt overwhelmed her. She should not be sleeping like that, not with so much on her mind, but then she remembered that she was still suffering jetlag and had not fully adjusted yet. She felt a little like a zombie must.

Stumbling from the bed, she found the bedside lamp and had to rub the sleep from her eyes before she could see the time on the clock. It was 5 a.m.

She had slept for hours; it had been nine when Ruthie insisted she went for a nap. Dragging on a robe, she wandered out into the house. One lamp was still on. Ruthie had gone back home, and a note propped up by the lamp asked her to call when she was up.

It was far too early to call Ruthie. She went into the kitchen and spooned coffee into the percolator, switched it on and sat at the kitchen table. She put her head in her hands, massaging her temples.

The aroma of freshly made coffee revived her somewhat. There were things she needed to do. Jack's family had to be notified. He did not get along with them but nevertheless his parents still loved him in their way.

She searched herself for some emotion but felt only drained. An overwhelming sadness arose inside her; it was all such a waste. What had happened to make things end in this tragedy? Was it her fault? Had she driven Jack away? Maybe she should not have agreed to come here. It had been his idea but she knew in her heart of hearts that Jack would not make a good immigrant. He was the wrong type of person. He was fond of the life he had. Whenever they had gone abroad he had complained that the place fell far short of his own country. That should have given her a clue, but no, she had gone along with it, because after her parents had been killed, she felt that she would like something different. A new country was a challenge and she liked a challenge.

In the silence, a door creaked open. As if paralyzed for a moment, she stayed in her chair, her hands cupped around the mug of steaming coffee. There was a whisper of movement. Taking hold of the coffee mug by the handle, she made herself stand and very quietly cross the kitchen floor. She peered around the door, ready to throw the mug and its contents at whoever was there.

A long shadow crossed the floor, heading towards the bedroom; she slid around the door and then almost fainted with relief. It was Job.

She whispered his name and he jumped a little, and then turned. 'You startled me,' he admitted, recrossing the room to join her. 'Thank you, I'll have that.' He took the beaker

161

and took a sip. 'Here, drink some.' He held it out for her. She also took a sip. 'There,' he murmured. 'Better?' Her eyes searched his face. His eyes had dark smudges beneath them. He looked overwrought, as if he had had a really hard time.

'It is . . .' She couldn't finish.

'Jack, yes, I'm afraid so. But you knew that, didn't you?'

'Sort of. They seemed too sure of themselves for it not to be him.'

He put an arm around her and led her to the sofa. 'Sit down,' he commanded.

She did so, asking, 'Did they have any more information?'

'None. But I think . . . call it intuition . . No, it's more than that. I think they suspect that I am involved.'

'That is ridiculous! How can they even think that?'

'Before we get into that, Bron, I want you to know that I didn't do anything to Jack.'

'You don't even have to say that, Job.'

He sat beside her and, taking up her hand, planted a tender kiss on the palm. 'Thank you for saying that, Bron. But you might change your mind because there is something that I haven't told you.'

Job was sleeping. While he was taking a shower, she had remade the bed for him and he more or less fell into it. 'Thanks, honey,' he murmured and was asleep very quickly. He slept like a man without anything on his conscience, just as she knew he would.

After a quick shower she dressed in jeans and a sweater and went out into the lounge. She called Jack's brother, knowing it would be a reasonable time in England. It was not something she wanted to do over the telephone but there was no other way. She thought it would be better if he were to tell their parents. He was devastated as she knew he would be.

'What happened?' Darren asked.

'I'm not sure yet,' then went on to tell his brother what she knew. He promised to be in touch, his parents might want to come over.

'That's fine, anything I can do I will.'

'You were a good wife to Jack,' Darren said. 'I'm sure he knew that.'

I am sure he didn't, she thought, but did not give voice to the words. There was no need to go into anything with Jack's family. Whatever she said, however she said it, the money, the gambling, the deceit, none of it would make Jack look good and she did not want to do that to his parents or his brother. They would never know the things he had done, and if she had her way it would never come out. It was between her and Jack and no one else. It was important that his parents had happy memories of their son. Even though Jack had not got on with them, they had always loved him and tried to be supportive. It was Jack who caused the trouble; the truth was he had been ashamed of his parents. They were honest-to-goodness working-class folks and he was not proud of that. He hated it that his brother drove a bus for a living, that his dad had gone down the pit. He never saw them as worthy. She had argued with him about it but had never got through to him. That should have told her something about his personality, but she had let it go. Young and in love, she realized she had forgiven an awful lot about Jack.

For the rest of the morning she kept busy as best she could, going over to Ruthie to let her know what had happened and then staying in the house and, in the end, taking the phone off the hook because there had been some calls from the press.

Mr Clarkson, the senior partner in the law firm that had sacked Jack, telephoned to offer condolences to her and also to let her know that the police had been to see him. He said the firm would help in any way they could and she should just call them.

She heard a car pull up outside and went to look through the shutters. She had kept them closed on the front just in case the press came in person. To her mortification she saw it was Marged getting out of a rental car. She was so disappointed to see her cousin that, until it was too late, she forgot that Job was in her bed.

'I heard about it, Bron, how terrible.' The blonde girl rushed to her side and took her in an embrace. Bron had the desire to wriggle free but stopped herself. 'I can't believe it,' Marged said, letting Bron go and putting her bag down. 'It was in the paper. I mean, to see it like that. I went to the police to make sure it was true.'

'Did you? Why didn't you call me?' Bron asked. She was suspicious of Marged. Could it have been her that had told the police about Job and Jack arguing? Marged said nothing, merely looking around the room as if she had mislaid something.

Deciding she could not prevaricate, Bron decided to be direct and said, 'Marged, I . . . Job's here. He's sleeping.'

'Oh?' the other girl's eyes widened.

'He's in my room. He went to Auckland to . . . well to identify Jack.'

'That was kind of him. How come he didn't stay there to sleep? He does have an apartment there, doesn't he?'

'Probably because he wanted to be with me,' Bron said, as mildly as possible.

The look that Marged gave her took Bron back to the

faraway past. It was pure Marged. A look she had not seen for a long while, sulky and spiteful somehow, and just as in the past, she said nothing and just stared for some long moments. Uncomfortable with that stare, as she had always been, Bron turned away, going into the kitchen. 'Would you like something to eat, or drink?'

The answer was a while coming. 'Coffee, please.' It was as if she had pulled a plug on her feelings, for Marged strode to her cousin's side and accompanied her into the kitchen. 'Bron, it's Mother all over again,' she said.

Bron froze. She had thought that only hours ago and had said as much to Ruthie. It was as if someone had put a curse on the family. But they were ordinary people, ordinary to the point of being boring, she thought. Not interesting enough for anyone to bother about putting curses on them. It was a horrible coincidence, there was no connection.

As she made the coffee, Bron told Marged what had happened in Wales. Marged was dismissive of any idea that it had to do with what happened to Jack. Her being attacked, now that was really coincidence. She also showed little sympathy but Bron was used to that. Bron was not sure but she thought that even a little fake sympathy would have been better than the cool way she handled it. It confirmed, if any confirmation was needed, what she had always known. If she had no love for Marged, then Marged had even less for her.

Marged went on evenly. 'You hear of that happening to lone women hikers. But you were lucky nothing *really* bad happened to you.'

Bron supposed she meant her being murdered or raped. But the choice of words 'really bad' seemed inappropriate. After all, she might have died had the shepherd not found her and having your skull smashed was somewhat momentous! However, she let it go, not wanting a prolonged discussion.

'So, I understand that Job went to identify Jack for you – and that was really kind – but what I don't quite understand is why he has to sleep here? How come he didn't go home?'

'I don't know why he didn't go home. I think perhaps he did not want me to be on my own.'

'Oh, I see, well, you're not on your own now, are you? You have me here. You could wake him and ask him to go home, surely?'

'No, I couldn't do that, Marged.' Bron sighed, dreading what she had to say and fearful of saying it badly. 'Firstly, he is exhausted and needs to sleep and the other thing is that Job . . .' She paused, straightened her spine and looked Marged in the eye. 'Job and I discovered that we were attracted to one another. We started a relationship.'

Marged lowered her long pale lashes over her eyes. She turned to one side, smoothing her hand along her skirt at the hip. 'I see,' she said at last. 'You mean he's . . .'

'Don't even go there!' Bron said, sensing what the girl had been going to say.

'I was going to say quite a dish.' She gave a funny little smile, but the smile did not light up her eyes. Bron knew she was lying and what was more she sensed, in the little gestures she made, that Marged knew that too.

'Oh, well, I suppose all is fair in love and war,' she murmured. 'I knew you liked him but you would never admit it, would you?'

'I didn't realize just how much until he came—' Bron stopped.

'Go on. Until he came where exactly? Or do you mean metaphorically?'

'What?' Bron clicked her tongue irritably. 'He came to Wales after my accident.'

'I see. So you told him but you didn't see fit to tell me.'

'I didn't want to worry you and there was nothing you could do. Besides, he offered. I didn't ask him or tell him. Ruthie did that.'

'Oh, she would!' Marged betrayed a soupçon of anger. At least, Bron thought, that was honest.

'Anyway, Job has been really kind to me.'

'I'm sure he has,' Marged said. 'He can be kind. If he likes you, of course. If he doesn't then better watch out. I think Jack found that out.'

'I'm sorry?'

Marged sniffed. 'Well . . .'

There was a movement and both women turned to the kitchen door. Job stood in the doorway. 'Well what, Marged? Don't let me stop you.'

'Nothing,' she murmured. 'You look dreadful, Job.'

'Yes, I know.' He ran a hand over his chin and cheek where stubble grew. 'Bron, I'm going to my place. I need some stuff. Thanks for the use of the bed. Two hours' sleep was fine.'

'It's not enough, Job,' she said to him. 'Do you want me to drive you home?'

'No, really, I'm OK.' He put a hand on her shoulder. 'But you can walk me to the car if you like.'

They reached his car, it had grown chilly and a wind danced through the trees, spiralling dead leaves into restless movement. The blue sky of earlier now looked washed out. Dark clouds with ominous slowness lumbered across the heavens.

'I can't stay with her around,' he said.

'I know. It makes it awkward.'

He tucked her hair behind her ears gently. 'You can come to my place later in the week. There's too much going on at the moment. Better not create gossip.'

'It is difficult, I know, but I still want to see you.'

'I'll sort something out – well, *we* will, I'll phone you on your cell. Bron, you know what I think?'

'No, I don't know what you think so you had better tell me.' She smiled up at him.

'I think that I'm head over heels in love with you and that is a first for me.'

She gasped, gazing up into his dark, fathomless eyes. 'Job, I . . . I don't know what to say.'

'Then don't say anything, honey. Wait until the time is right. You've been through hell but you will come out the other side and I'll be waiting.'

She raised her lips to his, kissing him softly. 'Thank you, for everything.'

Bron asked her cousin what she had been going to say the moment she got in the house. Marged had gone into the living room and was staring down at the floor by the French windows. 'What happened here?' she asked.

'I don't know.' Bron wanted to add, *You tell me*, but she didn't. There was nothing she could do to prove that Marged had scratched the floor. Things that had happened in the past came into her mind. Little inconsequential things, lost toys, books with pages torn or with something spilled on them. No one was caught actually doing it. Her mother had at first refused to blame Marged and said that Bron must have done it and forgotten. It was always Bron who had mislaid her toys. 'You're a scatty old thing,' her mother would say. And Bron always accepted it. Then it happened too often and even her mother had been suspicious of Marged. She felt so much sympathy for the girl that she never accused her. Perhaps she spoke to Aunt Lily about it, but she never said. Now she thought that perhaps, like the ruined floor, all the time it had been Marged and for no good reason. Perhaps she did it because she could make life a little unpleasant for her cousin. Bron snapped out of the reminiscence and asked again. 'What were you going to say before Job interrupted us?'

'Well, I don't like to really but I suppose I should. I was at the apartment and Job came to see Jack. Jack didn't let him in. They were outside in the passage and they were arguing.'

'Oh, really? What were they arguing about?'

'I can't be sure. I think it was to do with money. Did Jack owe Job money? Or was it the other way around?'

'Hardly the other way around. I told you about Jack's financial problems, Marged. It was a bad argument, was it?'

'Oh yes, I thought it was going to get violent.'

'Is that why you felt it your duty to tell the police about it?'

Red flooded Marged cheeks. It crept up from her neck, making her skin look as if it were on fire.

'Why would you say that?'

'Oh, come on, Marged. The police questioned Job about it today; he told me all about it. They said they had had a tip-off.'

'Well, what if I did? Don't you think the police should know?'

'I thought he was your friend.'

'Jack was my friend.' Marged's eyes narrowed, and her hands curled into fists at her sides. 'And we don't know Job Tepi really well, do we? How do we know what he's capable of? I mean, look at his sister and that drunk she's married to – he was hardly born into money, was he? Where does he get all his money from? Have you ever thought about it? I don't suppose you have. Just because he's some kind of stud, you think he's Mr Perfect, but I think he's a bit of a gangster.'

Bron thought she had never heard anything so ridiculous, or as mean-spirited. She decided not to credit the statement by giving an answer. Instead she murmured, 'If Jack owed Job money, he was hardly likely to kill him for it.'

'He could have done it for someone else.'

'A contract killer, do you mean? Job Tepi? Oh yes, I can see that. Let's just say, Marged, that I know more about it than you. You had no right to tell the police. It's made them suspicious about Job.'

'So you care more about Job Tepi than helping to find your husband's murderer.'

'That isn't true. I want Jack's murderer caught. I want him caught now . . . today! I want the police to find him and I don't want them chasing up false avenues because a very silly woman wanted to make trouble, or be part of the drama. Was that it, Marged, you wanted the attention?'

Marged stepped forward, and with hands bunched into fists and raised like a demented pugilist's, she charged into Bron, pushing her so hard that she lost her balance and fell on to the hardwood floor. It rammed into her hip, causing her to gasp with the pain. Her head was spinning, the loss of balance triggering something in her head that made her fearful of passing out.

'You're the silly bitch, not me! Letting him into your bed, just like the slut you always were. My mother was right about you! I thought you were my friend.' Marged raised

170

her foot, bringing it down with precision into Bron's side. The pain ricocheted through her but she could not drag herself up – she tried but fell back, and a rushing sound in her ears made her feel as if she would be sick. Fearing the girl would kick her again, she curled up into a ball, covering her head in her hands.

'I hate you, bitch. I always hated you!'

Bron came to; she felt cold and shivered. The pain at her side was still throbbing but the waves of dizziness had passed and the rushing in her ears was no more. It was fairly dark; the wind was driving the rain against the windows. Struggling to her feet, she reached first of all for the lamp and clicked it on and then listened to the silence beyond the noise of the storm. As quietly as she could manage, she lifted the receiver from the telephone. Her fingers trembled as she pressed the numbers.

'Tepi,' he answered quickly and very abruptly.

'Job . . . Job, come, please come . . . I . . . I don't know if she's still here . . .'

He did not question or delay. 'I'm on my way.'

Slowly she slid on to the settee. There was a bright yellow woollen throw over the back and she took it, wrapping it around her. Not certain whether she was cold or in shock, she hugged the throw to her.

'Bron . . .' She heard Ruthie's voice. Relief flooded through her as she called out to tell Job's sister where she was.

'What is it? Job phoned.' Ruthie was carrying a cricket bat, obviously as some kind of weapon and in spite of how she felt, Bron smiled a little. Ruthie was as practical and sensible as ever.

'I don't know if she's gone . . .'

'The car's gone,' Ruthie said. 'Let me check, are you OK?'

'No, no, Ruthie, I'm not.'

By the time Job arrived, Ruthie had made tea and lit the fire. They had examined Bron's side and found it bruised from the kick that Marged had given to her; the other side where she had slammed down on to the floor was sore but not discoloured. Bron refused a doctor. A cup of tea would be better help for her shock than any tranquilizer, she declared. She needed to keep her wits about her.

Job had not been at the hotel but at his home beyond Kaitaia; it had taken him a while to get down as the storm was pretty violent now. There had been trees blown over and one of the roads was flooded.

'What happened?' he asked, anxiously sitting beside her on the settee and taking up her hand. 'You look terrible, honey. Has something—'

'*Her* and you might know it,' Ruthie interrupted. 'She attacked her.'

'Who do you mean? Marged? What the hell is going on?'

'I didn't realize that she hated me so much.'

Bron squeezed his hand, still trying to come to terms with the vicious attack on her by her cousin. 'I knew we didn't get on that well . . . but she hates me, I mean, really hates me. It's not just you, Job, I mean not just because of us, but more than that. And it was her – she told the police about your argument with Jack. She was there, at the apartment . . .'

'He said she had left, a week back. Why was he lying about that?'

'Job, do you think they were having an affair? Was that it?'

'Who knows? She's sly enough. Let me call the doctor, honey?'

'No, really, if I feel bad tomorrow then I'll see him, but I don't want him coming out on a night like this. There's no good reason for it. I'm all right now, I'm just in shock. Ruthie looked after me really well.'

Ruthie left them, promising to make them some dinner. 'Come over or if you're not up to it, I'll bring it here. Just rest, Bron, and Job, don't you go off.'

'Horses and elephants won't get me out of here,' he assured her.

They sat for a while, trying to understand what had happened to make Marged lose her control. It made no sense. She was out of control. Bron had never known the woman to be violent before. Perhaps she had had to submerge her character for so long, being dominated by her mother, that now with her mother dead, she was just releasing all her pent-up frustration.

'I think she needs help,' Job said. 'If she comes back we have to get her to see someone – there's obviously some-thing the matter with her. I could feel sorry for her. In fact, I did once, but now she's done this to you . . . Well, I can't feel anything but anger.'

'And she told tales on you too. I can't understand why she would want to get you into trouble, Job. I thought she was crazy about you.'

'May I remind you of the girl who scratched my car? Sometimes fascination can turn to hate very quickly.'

'You shouldn't be such a dish,' she managed to say lightly.

'I know but I can't help it. I'm going to run you a bath. It will do you good, help those bruises.'

'Thank you, Job.'

He leaned over her, kissing her lips very gently. 'I'm going to make sure you are never left on your own again.'

'You have to leave me sometime. But don't worry, I have Ruthie's cricket bat and no one is going to attack me again without getting it back – twofold!'

CHAPTER TEN

THE weeks crawled by, the winter storms giving way to early spring rain and sun and rain again. The chill was fading away into mildness. Flowers burst from the rich soil and fruit trees were heavy with blossom. Bron watched it all with a sense that nothing was real any more. Nothing had come to light about what had happened to Jack. An inquest stated that he had been killed by a person or persons unknown. The police had no clues.

However, things had been really difficult. The investigation had left her feeling dirty. The detective had trawled through her private life. How long had she been in a relationship with Job Tepi? Had Jack known? Was that why he had left? Questions and interviews and all asked with a faint sneer. She knew he had not believed her. He so obviously thought she had been seeing Job behind Jack's back. *As if!* Nothing she said in connection with Jack's disappearance seemed to have any bearing on the case. The fact that Jack had tricked her, taken all her money, sold the boat from under her, none of it mattered. All that seemed to interest him was the fact that she was sharing a bed with Job Tepi. That was his only point of investigation, or so it seemed.

Job was interviewed for longer than her, and in the end they came up with a witness who said he had seen Jack after the time that Job had his altercation with him. After that date Job had been back at home, so there were plenty of people to alibi him. Not that that mattered. Job was still under suspicion and so was she. It was a nice convenient situation: the lovers planned to kill the deluded husband. She knew that was what Cartwright thought even though he did not come out and say it.

Somehow the size ten boots stomping through her life had destroyed the magic. She knew she could not see Job again. It was, she thought, a sordid little affair. That was how the police saw it and she had started to see it that way too.

Jack had been murdered and she had been carrying on with a man who could have been involved. She didn't know where that had come from but the thought persisted. Job had not murdered Jack but the thought that he knew more than he said just would not go away. It was ridiculous, her sane mind screamed at her, but something nagged. A thing that was instinctive and primeval. It stemmed from the detective; he had hinted at something that he knew but could not reveal.

Marged had not come back. In fact Bron had not heard from her since she had left and neither had Job. Knowing it was she who had told the police about Job's argument with Jack, Bron had asked the police if they had an address for their witness but they refused to give it to her.

She tried to explain that Marged was her cousin, that she did not want to harm her but wanted only to give her some belongings she had left behind.

'She will come for them if she needs them,' the policeman told her. He had instructions from higher up that the witness had not wanted her address to be given to anyone and especially *not* her cousin.

'How strange,' she murmured. But perhaps not. After all, Marged might think she had a score to settle with her. Nothing was further from the truth; all Bron wanted was her clothes and trinkets out of her house. She did not tell the police that Marged had attacked her. That seemed so far away and irrelevant. The attack was caused by jealousy; it had nothing to do with Jack or anything else.

Finally, Bron packed Marged's belongings in a cardboard box, sealed it with strong tape, placed it in two large plastic garbage sacks and put it on the shelf that ran around one wall of the garage. In a way it was what she would also be doing to Job. She would pack him up and put him in the garage of memories.

He had never mentioned the four-letter word since that one time. Anyway, when he had said it, he had qualified it. I *think*, he had said, not I am. There had been no positive there. She need not feel guilty. He had wanted to see her but she had been putting him off. Things to do at school, she was tired, she had a cold. Any excuse so as not to see him.

'Oh, Jack,' she murmured into the stillness. 'What happened to you? What did you do that made your life so . . .' She sighed. Whatever he had done, either to her or to anyone else, the last thing he deserved was to be murdered. No one deserved that. He had been her friend, her husband, her companion over the years. They had had fun. As students, life had been carefree. Neither could ever have imagined how their relationship would end. If she had asked to point to anyone whose life would end so miserably, then Jack would have been the last one she would have considered. Into what dark alley had he turned to deserve that? Would she ever know?

Telling Job had been easier than she had imagined. She asked to meet him, not at the house or at his hotel, somewhere – and she stressed the word – neutral. He suggested the marina, his boat. 'I don't want to go out,' she said.

'Not a problem,' he said. Was he cool? He sounded different but then again maybe she sounded different too and he was only echoing her tone of voice.

It was an unexpectedly warm day; there was no breeze and the water lay flat calm. It was not a day for sailing. Job had not bothered to unfurl the sails on the motor-sailer and by the way he was dressed, he had no plans for sailing that day.

He was sitting on deck at the small foldaway table, a coffee pot and two cups already set out. She saw him before he had seen her and for a moment she studied him. Her heart gave a little lurch, her stomach an even bigger one. Each sensitized part of her stirred into life. There was feeling even at the back of her eyes, a faint tingling as his appearance gave delight to her. She thought of how it had been, the fun and the pleasure and the laughter. The detective's sneer came into her mind and it obliterated every one of the feelings.

'Job.' She merely murmured his name but he heard. He stood in a fluid, contained movement and stretched out a hand to help her on board. She said she would be all right – knowing that his touch would undo her determination to end their relationship.

He shoved his hand into the pocket on his lightweight jacket, as if it had been offensive to her. Oh Job, she thought, if only you knew.

'Coffee?' he asked. She glanced up at him. His expression

told her nothing.

'No, well, yes, of course.'

Uncomfortably she slid into the seat and let him pour the black liquid into her cup. 'This is fine,' she murmured, refusing cream.

'I know you like it black,' he said, pouring cream into his own cup.

'Job, I don't know how to say this but I . . .' she paused.

'Sure you can say it, Bron, you have it all planned.'

'No, I don't.' She felt her cheeks burn. 'I am not that calculating. Job, I'm sorry, I just don't want to see you any more.'

'That will be difficult, unless you're moving away.'

'You know what I mean!'

'Yes, I do. Sorry.' He stood, again that controlled movement, his face an unreadable mask. 'If that's all, I have somewhere to be. Finish your coffee.'

He turned away, swaying purposely to the ladder and then swinging himself down on to the pontoon. It was done so quickly that he was gone before she fully realized that he meant it.

Bron left her seat and went to lean over the side of the boat. She saw him striding across the car park and watched until he dropped from sight.

What had she expected? That he would plead with her to change her mind, that he would be unpleasant? But no, Job had too much pride for that. Perhaps they had been two people at the right time after all and it had been good but it was at an end, its end maybe satisfying both partners.

She went back and sat down, sipping her coffee. If it was right why did she feel so crushed and hollow and beaten? Emotionally she was drained. It was the right thing to do – what they had shared had been sullied.

When she arrived back Ruthie was on the front porch. It was obvious to Bron that Ruthie had seen her but her friend went inside without acknowledging Bron's wave. The reaction of Ruthie was in some respects more upsetting than Job's had been. She knew she had lost a friend. Ruthie had taken sides. Job must have called her.

Life was lonely. After school she drove home and, unless she went to the dairy or to the RSA club, she had no one to talk to. Although Ruthie would acknowledge her and say hello, it was perfectly clear by her attitude that that was as far as it would go. Pride and sensitivity for Ruthie's feelings made it impossible for Bron to explain why she had ended it with Job. His sister loved him and was proud of him, it was too much to expect her to understand why Bron had tossed him to one side.

The house she had so loved became her prison and she started to consider moving away. But to where? Auckland? But that was not far enough away and there were memories there of Jack's miserable fate. Wellington seemed a possibility, or maybe South Island. Yet she was not really serious about moving.

Restless and miserable, she walked down to the bottom of the garden. The warm scents of spring were all around her. It was November but delicious, in England it would be cold and grey and winter. She had hated November when she had lived there and now, at the other side of the world, she looked forward to the month as the pre-emptor of spring.

It would soon be Christmas and the long break from school. Lazy summer days.

It was very quiet; not even the hum of a car's engine broke the silence. Ruthie's house was in darkness so she guessed they had gone out somewhere. Gazing back at the house, she saw the one table lamp glowing through the darkness. *There was a shadow.* Bron started, moved back deeper into the garden, her heart starting to accelerate. There was a large bush; she slipped behind it, peering back at the window. There was nothing there, just the amber glow of the lamp. But no, there was a shadow – thin and black. *Someone was in the house.*

Nervously, she looked around, then, crouching low, crossed the grass into Ruthie's garden. She sped across the lawn and then out on to the road. There was no car parked in the road. Whoever was in her house had come on foot.

It was very dark now, and the one street lamp was not working. The grass looked black and was barely illuminated by the stars. Going out into the road, she headed away from her house, running now along the street. The dairy was still open; a shaft of light illuminated the pavement. She dived in, startling Mr Connor, who was obviously just about to close.

'Where's the fire?' he moaned as she sped to a halt.

'Someone's in my house,' she said breathlessly. 'I need to phone the police.'

'Are you sure you need to do that, Bron? It might be Ruthie or . . .' He hesitated and the blood ran into his rather bulbous nose. Obviously he had been going to say Job. Everyone had to know about her and Job and their past intimacy! Uncomfortable as she was with the thought, she brushed it out of her mind. She could not deal with that now. Now there were more frightening things to worry about than gossip.

'It might be Marged come back,' he said, recovering from his embarrassment.

'Without a car?'

'There's no car? Well, it has to be kids.'

'Kids? Kids don't do that around here, go into people's homes. Look, can I use the phone or not?'

She recognized the policeman as the one who had come with the detective. He had been more pleasant than the odious Cartwright. His name was Rickard. Curtis Rickard. He was new to the area, transferred from the city, but people rather liked him.

'Mrs Mellor,' he said. 'What's the problem?'

Bron told him: a shadow, that was all she saw, but it told her that someone was in her house. She was aware that Mr Connor had raised his eyebrows at the constable, and as he did not know her, the constable could be forgiven for thinking that she did this kind of thing all the time.

Considering that hardly anyone in town knew Jack, or those that did barely liked him, it was startling to realize that some viewed her with suspicion as well. Mr Connor obviously was one of those. He had never been the same since it had all come out about Jack. Small town, small minds, Jack used to say, but she had thought him dreadfully wrong. She had loved the people in town. Only now she saw there was perhaps something in what he had said. It was not paranoia but she knew that people were talking about her. She could tell in the supermarket or at the RSA club. She had even stopped going to the club because of it. No one said anything to her, exactly – in fact, they were as pleasant as always – but they still talked about her. Hardly surprising: not many women could claim to have had a husband who had been murdered and then thrown in the ocean. She was more than a nine-day wonder, and her relationship with Job had not helped either. They probably, like the police, assumed it had been going on a long time.

'OK,' Curtis Rickard said, 'we'll go back there and I'll take a look around.'

He put her in the back of the car. When they reached the road he parked closer to Ruthie's house, which was still in darkness. She tried to open the door but it was locked. The constable turned in his seat. 'I have to unlock it,' he murmured.

'I'm hardly a felon.' She could not stop snapping out the words. 'I am actually a victim here!'

He shrugged but made no excuse. He released the lock; she heard it click and tumbled out. 'Don't you go into the house, you stay here,' he said, when he joined her.

He sidled up to the house. In moments he was gone from her sight. There was once more the ominous silence and then light flooded across the lawn as the constable switched on lights.

He was out in the porch in seconds and called out to her. 'There's no one here. You can come in now.'

The doors that led into the kitchen and the bedrooms were open so he had obviously been in every room.

'Did you look into the closets?' she asked. The house had walk-in closets.

'Look,' he said, 'I'm not an idiot.'

'I didn't say you were. I thought you might not know about the closets.'

'I've been here before, remember.' He was very terse. Of course, they had come and looked around the house in their pursuit of Jack's murderer. Rather, they had come looking for something to tie either her or Job into Jack's killing.

'I had forgotten,' she said. 'There was someone here. I didn't imagine it.'

Curtis Rickard shrugged. 'But there's no one here now,' he said. 'If I were you I would keep your doors and windows locked. It could have been an opportunist druggie.'

'What? Here? In this town?' she questioned aghast.

'You'd be surprised at what happens in this town.'

'Yes, I would if you're saying there are drug addicts and thieves.'

'You don't know everyone in town or on the outskirts. Believe me, there are not loads of bad people but there are some. Everyone has their share of these villains. Just because you don't see them doesn't mean they aren't around.'

She said miserably, 'I thought I had found the one place where I'd never have to lock my doors.'

'Those days have gone everywhere,' he said. 'No, I guess I am being unfair. Generally you are OK up here, but you never know.' Then, seeming to feel a little more disposed to her, he asked, 'Will you be all right now?'

'Yes. I'm sorry I was a trouble to you.'

'No problem. It's my job. Lock the door after me, Mrs Mellor.'

'I will.'

He stepped out on to the porch, then turned back. 'What about Job Tepi?'

'What about him?'

'I thought he stayed here. He could protect you.'

She hesitated, not sure whether he was being sarcastic or nosey. 'He doesn't stay here any more,' she murmured. 'I'm on my own now.'

'Well, take care.'

He turned and sauntered away into the darkness. Quickly she shut the door and turned the key. She took the key from the lock, and tested the lock before going from room to room checking windows and shutting those that were open. She had never felt it necessary to lock a window, and the task made her even more depressed. The last job was to make sure that the door that led into the garden was locked. She listened into the night but there was no sound. The silence was unnerving.

What was the matter with her? She had never been the jumpy type but then again, that was before someone had attacked her in Wales . . . and before her husband had been murdered. Now she was nervous and edgy, her confidence weakened by all that had happened to her. She almost gave into tears but she shook herself out of that, biting her lower lip hard before she strode to the kettle to turn it on and set about making a camomile tea.

Taking the cup when it was ready she went to her bedroom and undressed, slipping into pyjamas before climbing into bed and settling down to read and to occasionally take a sip of tea.

Somewhere she had read the description 'the silence was deafening'. She had wondered what that meant and now she knew. The silence was like thunder, pounding away at her, her ears pricked and alert. If she were a dog, she thought those ears of hers would be pinned right back, listening . . . listening for what? There was nothing and no one, not even a scratching or the creak of furniture, no rustle of the wind whispering through the trees or tip-tapping against the window panes. Finding it impossible to read, she finished her tea and lay down in the bed, pulling the duvet up over her head.

She was coughing, that was what had wakened her. Drowsily she pulled the duvet from her face. The first thing she became aware of was the smell, thick and acrid. It took a moment of more coughing for her to realize something was terribly wrong. She searched for the light. Clouds of black smoke were billowing into the room from beneath the door. *Fire!*

Vaulting from the bed, she ran to the door. The handle was hot; she withdrew her hand, spat on the palm and put her hand on it again. The door failed to open. She tugged at it, feeling panic well up inside her. The door was stuck, or worse, it was locked, locked from the other side.

She sped across the room to the window, realizing as she tugged at it that she had locked it – *and the keys were in the main part of the house*. What an idiot.

'Keep calm,' she muttered to herself, but she was coughing and the smoke was burning her eyes. The smoke was black and toxic. Through the plumes she looked for something with which to break the window. She remembered she had heard about keeping low on the floor. She fell to her knees, then lay flat, finding herself able to breathe a little better. She crawled snake-like towards the closet. What she needed was a shoe – a stiletto.

Job said, 'I don't like that you are doing this, Ruthie. It has nothing to do with you and you shouldn't take sides.'

Ruthie gazed up at him, a little fazed by this attitude. 'You can't tell me that after what she did to you!'

'She dumped me. It was her privilege to do that.'

'Not like she did it. Look, Job, I think it was unforgivable. Everyone knew you had been picked up by the police. That you were a suspect in Jack Mellor's death. Her dumping you like she did, well, it looks like there was something in it. People have said so. It made you look like you knew more about it than could be proven.'

'People are stupid, Ruthie. It was nothing to do with that, it was emotional. Bron wasn't in love with me. What we had was just one of those things.'

'That's bull, and you know it. It meant a lot to you. Tell me, have you ever been *dumped* before?'

'What's that got to do with anything?'

'It's got everything to do with it. Who in their right mind would dump you? You have everything going for you!'

He smiled, shrugging his broad shoulders. 'Ruthie, maybe I have but you can't force someone to like you because you have *everything* going for you. What concerns me is you and Bron. You were such mates – don't let me come between you.'

'You're not mates with her.'

'I might be,' he murmured. 'One day. First I have to get over her and I'm nowhere near there yet. Once that happens I'll offer the hand of friendship. But you need to do that now. The girl needs you. God, Ruthie, think what she's been through. She must be feeling so lonely. They all talk about her – the woman whose husband was murdered. I've heard them. It must be dreadful for her. OK, I admit she hurt me but like I said, you can't make someone stay with you if they don't want.'

'Oh, Job. I could hit her, I really could.'

'Ruthie, I'm a big boy now. I don't need you to fight my battles.'

He put his arm around her and gave her a deep hug. She looked at him with adoring eyes. He was and always would be her little brother. He was the youngest and the most precious in the family. She had all but brought him up, their parents had had to work day and night to earn the money to keep them fed and clothed. It had been hard. They had been so poor. She remembered pushing Job in the sixth-hand trolley when he was a baby; his clothes well past their wearable date.

Job would go to school shoeless and not because he

preferred it but because he grew so fast that he had soon outgrown the new shoes his parents had got for him.

His behind had not quite hung out of his britches but he had never had the trendy clothes the other kids had. He had to fight his way out of that scenario and when he could not fight them, Ruthie took over for him.

No one had given Job Tepi anything. Everything he had achieved he had done on his own. She did not know how and never asked. He left home, he earned money, and he came back. He worked some more and he earned more and now . . . well, now he had everything. Everything except the woman he loved.

'Adam's been imbibing and you had some champagne. I'll drive you home. Leave the car here – you can get it tomorrow.'

'You're a good boy.' She patted his cheek lightly. 'And I'd appreciate that. Let's get Adam home. It's been a lovely evening, thanks, Job.'

'My pleasure.'

It was his sister's wedding anniversary and Job had surprised them by arranging a dinner at his hotel. Everything had been perfect. Adam had insisted on driving himself but then had found it difficult to refuse the temptation of alcohol. Job worried about that aspect of his brother-in-law's personality, but Ruthie always assured him it was never a problem. He liked to drink sometimes but not all the time. Besides, he was happy when he was drunk, so she had learned to accept it.

It was late, the streets were deserted and all was still and quiet. Before parking he glanced almost automatically towards Bron's house. There was light flickering at the windows. He looked again. *God!* Flinging open the car door, Job sprinted across the lawn, yelling back at the confused couple that it was fire. Bron's house was on fire.

The front of the house was blazing, and he knew if he opened the front door he would cause even more of an inferno. He charged around the house to where the bedroom was along the porch. He was calling her name, and then Adam was at his side. He passed an axe to Job and Job smashed the window.

Black smoke spiralled out but ignoring Adam's warning, Job scrambled over the sill, feeling shards of glass tearing at his trouser legs. He ignored the pain of a jagged piece of glass that penetrated the material. He called again, and then unable to see anything he felt something against his foot. Throwing himself down, pulling off his shirt to cover his mouth, he felt Bron's body. She was retching but she was awake, in her hand a stiletto shoe. Dragging her, he crawled back to the window, and taking the shoe from her unresisting hand he quickly smashed out the remaining glass. Adam, sober now, grabbed Bron and pulled her through the opening. She gagged and gasped at the air as Adam pulled her away from the billowing smoke, then as her body hit the lawn, she heard the sound of the fire engine and saw Job scramble through the window. To the side of him she saw now the red-hot licking flames seeming to run along the wooden frame of the house. It was the last thing she remembered.

CHAPTER ELEVEN

BRON breathed in the pure oxygen through the mask, yet she could still smell smoke. It was oozing from her pores, and from her hair. She longed to stand under a shower to wash it away.

The doctor said she had been very lucky; there was no permanent damage to her lungs, her blood pressure was good and there was no circulatory damage. Job had been worse than her. They had done a bronchoscopy on him but he would be all right, given time.

Odd that, because Job had less time in the smoke than she had. 'I can't say why that is, but there are reasons,' the doctor said, then turned and walked away, obviously so she could not ask any more questions.

Guilt overwhelmed her. It was *all* her fault. The way she had treated Job and yet he had come to her rescue. He had not hesitated for a moment, a fireman had told her, and if he hadn't taken that dangerous decision, then it was pretty certain she would not have made it.

The black smoke was lethal. It came, the fireman explained, from the burning of some foam. She slid the mask to one side. 'But I don't have any foam like that. I was careful about buying furniture that did not contain anything like that. It's one of the things I am funny about.'

'Well, where do you think it came from?'

She moved her head on the pillow, slipping the mask back in place to take in further breaths of the wonderful oxygen.

'I shouldn't be talking to you, Bron. I just wanted to know how you were doing.'

She nodded, reached out and squeezed his hand.

'Thank you,' she managed.

'It isn't me you need to thank, it's Job Tepi.'

Oh Job, she thought, why? What is happening? I knew there was someone in the house. Rickard hadn't found them but they had to be there. It was no accident. Someone wanted her dead and that someone was *not* Job Tepi!

She dozed for a while after the fireman had left. Her eyes fluttered open to see Ruthie sitting in the chair at the side of her bed. Bron felt such relief it overwhelmed her. She savoured the moment before whispering her friend's name. Ruthie heard and left the chair.

'How are you?' she asked, putting her strong brown fingers around Bron's wrist.

'Better, better for seeing you.' Bron moved the mask. 'Oh, Ruthie, I . . .'

'No.' Ruthie adjusted the mask. 'Don't talk. I was a stupid moll. I'm sorry. You and Job, what you had – well, it's nothing to do with me. You're my friend and he's my brother, that's all that matters. I shouldn't have taken sides, I see that now.'

'Ruthie.' Determinedly Bron pushed at the mask, holding it in her hand so Ruthie could not push it back. 'I felt, I don't know . . . That policeman, raking over my life. I didn't suspect Job of anything, I just . . . I mean, I couldn't . . . Oh God, I don't know . . .' Tears spilled out of her eyes.

'For goodness' sake, girl, forget it. It's all in the past. Job made me see that. Please take the oxygen, I'll do the talking.' Ruthie waited till Bron did as she urged. 'All my life I looked out for him – I can't seem to break the habit – but he made me see how stupid I was being. I can't rule his emotional life and I can't make you love him if you don't want to. I was upset too, because people were gossiping – as they do – saying there was no smoke without fire ...'

'I think that's ironic!' Bron managed with a smile.

'Well, yeah, I think so too. Forgive me?'

Bron reached out and squeezed her hand. 'There's nothing to forgive, Ruthie, nothing at all, and as for Job – well, I guess he's my hero too!'

The house was a blackened ruin. A temporary fence had been erected to keep out the curious. Contractors would come to demolish it any day.

'I was never into property or things, but this just about breaks my heart,' Bron said to Ruthie. 'My own fault, I guess, for loving this house so much.'

'Nonsense, none of this is your fault, Bron. You must be really down to think that.'

'I think I am. I can't see how much more I can take. I'm usually so optimistic. Well, I used to be. Now ...' She sighed. 'Let's not stay here, Ruthie, I need to get away from the sight and smell.'

They crossed the grass and went into Ruthie's house. From the back you could not see the ruin that Bron's home had become. It was good to be out in the fresh air, sitting in the garden in the soft warm air of summer. Christmas was days away. She remembered the Christmas before when she had gone with Jack to Nelson. It had been a disaster because of his drinking. She had thought he was spiralling out of control then, but she had had no idea just how devastating their lives would turn out to be.

'How is Job? When they let me up I went to his room but he had gone.'

'He's OK. A bit weaker than you but he would not stay in the hospital. He has gone to the top end. You know he has a place up there.'

'Yes but I've never seen it.'

'Few people have. I guess I'm honoured. He hides away up there. He needs to. Those bloody cops have been hounding him again.'

'What? How could they? He saved my life. They don't think he started the fire?'

'No, they don't think that. Although Carty would like to think there was something he did.'

'Carty?'

'Cartwright.'

'You *know* him?'

' 'Course I do, everyone knows him up here. He comes from here. He always was a sneaky little bastard.'

'Ruthie!' In spite of the conversation, Bron laughed. Ruthie was not one to swear but something about Cartwright seemed to have wound her up.

'Well, he is. He was at school with Job, a year or two ahead of him, if I remember. He tried to bully Job. You know Job and me, and the rest of us, we were quite poor. Carty was an only child, had everything. Anyway, he tried to bully Job, but Job won't let anyone pick on him. He handled it and if he hadn't, well then I would have handled it for him. That's how we were – one tribe. You hit one, you hit us all.'

'I wish I had known all this before,' Bron sighed, realizing that Carty had to have an agenda. She had played right into his hands too.

'I wanted to tell you but Job wouldn't let me. If Carty thinks he can get something on Job he will try his best to make it stick. But he can't blame the fire on Job. Even that blockhead knows that if Job started a fire he's hardly likely to rescue the person that it's meant to . . . sorry Bron.'

'Don't worry; I know it was meant for me. The fireman told me it was deliberate, then Carty.' She smiled at her own use of the diminutive. 'Well, he told me too. I'm scared, Ruthie, because I don't know who or why. But I'm scared for Job, because it looks like Carty's trying to do something bad to Job as well.'

'He can't do anything. He can just make life unpleasant for Job but my brother can handle himself and if Carty goes too far, well, Job has friends too. And I do mean friends in the police.'

Ruthie offered to let Bron stay with her but Bron knew she needed a more permanent address. The house could be rebuilt but she was not sure she even wanted to live there any more. There was a small house for rent in the centre of town. Somehow she felt she would be safer there. The police were going to keep a close eye on her but they could not offer full protection.

They advised her to move away but she felt that would be far worse. After all, at least here she knew people. In a strange place she would have to start over and she was really in no mood to make new friends. She had lost her trust in people and that would be a long time getting back.

When school called her on her cell and asked her to go and see the headteacher, she had a feeling something was wrong. Driving back from the meeting, she knew she had been right to be apprehensive.

The school offered a long leave of absence – not quite a

suspension because she had done nothing wrong, but it more or less meant the same thing. She was not welcome there: she carried a threat to the pupils and many parents had been in to complain. It hurt.

Her whole life was crumbling and she could do nothing to stop the erosion.

In the end she offered to resign. Besides, she did not feel she would ever go back there again; it may be that she would leave the area eventually, if whoever was doing this to her was found. She had thought about changing her life and now she had the opportunity. A clean break would do her good.

In the event the package they offered was fair and reasonable and she would be able to keep herself for a couple of months if she were careful.

When she arrived back at Ruthie's she saw a familiar car on the drive. Her heart gave a skip and a jump, her stomach moving with that familiar lurching she had always experienced when she thought about Job Tepi. Now it was more intense. She felt excited too, she had not seen him since the fire. There was so much she needed to say.

Controlling herself, she strolled up the drive when all she wanted to do was run.

'Job,' she murmured, smiling at him. She felt the blood run up her neck, causing her face to turn red. 'How are you?'

He was standing, leaning against the worktop in the kitchen. Ruthie was sitting at the kitchen table but when she saw Bron, Job's sister stood and quietly left the room. She had gone before Bron realized what she had done.

'I'm OK. How are *you*?'

'Me? Oh, fine, scared,' she shrugged. 'Apprehensive, forever looking over my shoulder . . . Oh, Job you can't imagine how grateful I am . . .'

'Steady on.' He smiled. 'I only did what anyone would do.'

'Oh yes, I'm sure. You saved my life.'

'I wouldn't go that far.' He looked uncomfortable. His modesty warmed her heart.

'Well, that's what the fireman said.'

'They have a tendency to exaggerate, goes with the territory. Seriously, Bron, how are you?'

She could not lie to him. 'Physically I'm fine but mentally, fragile just about sums it up. But I have to keep going, Job, I can't let them get to me. I can't crack up, but it's difficult. I just got booted from school!'

'What?'

The words spilled out of her, she had forgotten how easy it was for her to communicate with him. They had always been able to talk to one another, from their first meeting.

He was furious about it, as she knew he would be. It offended his sense of fair play.

'I could tell them a thing or two,' he muttered, 'but I suppose you wouldn't let me. Ruthie says you're going to rent on East Street. Why don't you let me get you a room at the hotel? You'd feel safer, I'm sure, than being on your own.'

'I couldn't do that, Job. I need to be able to cook for myself. I wouldn't feel comfortable living in a hotel. It's a busy street and I have neighbours close by. I'm sure I'll be OK.'

'Well, it's up to you but think about it carefully.'

'A few of the neighbours I know from the RSA. They're nice people.'

'Sure, I know them too.'

He straightened. He looked slimmer somehow. Now she looked really hard at him he looked a little pale too. 'Are you sure you're OK? The doctor said you were worse than me. He didn't say why.'

'It's nothing.' He shrugged, considered and then said, 'I had lung trouble when I was a kid. I'm over it now but the weakness is always there.'

'Oh, Job.' She went to him, running a hand down his arm until she found his hand. Her eyes, she knew, were filled with tears but she could not help it. 'I'm sorry, for everything. I was such a . . . I don't know what I was. A fool hardly seems an adequate description.'

'Don't be concerned about it. You have enough to worry about.' Job had stiffened a little so she let his hand go, seeing too how he moved slightly away from her. It was wounding but she could understand it. He had to be over her now. He would not want her touching him.

'I need to talk to you, Bron, but not here. I don't want to involve Ruthie. Will you come with me? We can drive out somewhere, have a drink or something.'

'Of course. Job, it's nothing bad, is it?'

'No, but I have to tell the police, only I didn't want to tell Carty. He has it in for me and it makes me look bad.'

She looked up at him. He looked strained, as if he needed to rest. Part of her, the compassionate side, wanted to tell him to do that, but the other curious cat side had call on her too. In the end compassion won and she urged him to leave it. There was plenty of time.

'I can't. Every second I leave it means that the people who want to hurt you are out there. The cops are looking in the wrong direction and I need them to know that.'

Job drove south along the coast till they came to a small town. He parked and they crossed to a small roadside café. It was bright and cheerful inside but they went into the garden area. Huge kauri trees sheltered them from the sun

197

but it was still warm and comfortable.

He ordered tea after asking her what she wanted. They waited until the waiter brought their beverages before they talked. There were warm scones dripping with rich local butter that she found irresistible. She took one, and it was delicious, sweet and fruity. Job did not eat anything, just poured a cup of tea for her and one for himself. He seemed very troubled and Bron wondered what it was he had to say, what terrible secret he carried and why he thought Carty would use it against him.

'Ruthie told me about Carty. He made me feel bad about everything. I did not know he had an agenda. I let him manipulate me into thinking we had done something wrong. He made it all seem . . .' She paused, seeking a word. 'Grubby, I guess.'

'Carty always has an agenda. He can't forgive me for beating him in the playground. Bullies hate it when you take away their power. Little Job Tepi doing that to him robbed him of that superiority. I suppose he got a bit of it back being in the police.'

'If I had known all—'

'Look, Bron, let's not go there. It's all in the past. We have to forget it.'

She knew her eyes would reflect her hurt so she looked down and away from him. Taking up a piece of scone, she put it in her mouth, rolling it around on her tongue. Her throat felt hot with a burning sensation. She had done this to him; she had made him not want her any more.

He had had to get over her and it was final for him. That was what she had to deal with now. It was a disaster of her making. He was not going to get involved with her again, probably he imagined her to be mercurial and not to be trusted. She changed too often for him to take her seriously.

'Bron,' he began. He spoke slowly as if wanting to make certain that she understood everything. As far as he knew, he told her, there were no other debtors. He was the only one that Jack owed money to now. She could hardly believe him. Was he saying that he had made it all up, that there were no evil creditors stalking Jack?

'You mean there was no one else?'

'No, of course not. There were other guys but they aren't there now. I sorted them out.'

'But why didn't you tell me? Did you think I'd be angry with you?'

'Well, you were, but that wasn't why I didn't tell you. I paid them off. It seemed the easiest thing to do – to get them off your back, not Jack's. I did it for you. Anger I can deal with, Bron, but you are a woman of high principles. I was afraid you would insist on paying me back and I simply did not want you to do that. I went and bought out Jack's debts, that's all. I know now it wasn't them that went after you; they said they wouldn't do that. But they were going to go, in a legal way, after whatever assets you had, and that was your house, Bron. I didn't want them to take that from you.'

'Oh, Job.' Her hand reached out to his but then she withdrew it bearing in mind what he had said, he would not want her touching him at all. The offending hand she put on her lap, letting the other hand join it. The fingers of her right hand were stained with butter and she reached for a napkin to wipe them clean, Too late, she noticed, a small oily stain already impregnated her denim skirt.

'How much?'

'It doesn't matter now,' Job said.

'Of course it matters. I can pay you something. Surely you will let me do that?'

199

'You owe me nothing.'

'I owe you my life!'

'No, you don't. It was Jack's debt and that's where it stays, with Jack. The important thing, though, the thing that frightens me . . .'

'Yes?' She murmured in the wake of his silence.

'He had an insurance policy on your life. It was valued at about 50,000 English pounds. He offered to let them have it in lieu of his debt; they didn't take it. He told them they could do with it what they wanted and I think you might get the implication. But they didn't see the point of it. They are not into killing people.'

The negative that she omitted sounded strangled. 'No.' Then anger came rolling in but anger at Job and not at Jack. '*He wouldn't do that!*'

'If you don't believe me, you can check. I have the company's name. That policy has to be somewhere; you need to ask if he gave it to someone else, someone who is not as fond of you as I am. Someone who doesn't even know you or care about you. I have to go to the police with this, Bron. After the fire I can't prevaricate. I've thought about it for a long time. It seems you did not know Jack as well as you thought. He was a desperate man and a desperate man plans evil deeds. I'm sorry, Bron, but it is the truth.'

The urge to defend Jack rose up inside but only for several long and anguished moments. When it plummeted down inside her, she was weakened by it. Raising her elbows to the table, she buried her head in her hands, pushing back her hair. She had come to realize that she did not know Jack. The Jack she thought she knew would never have done these things. He had, through some need to bring reckless excitement into his life, allowed himself to spiral out of control. Yet she needed to strike out at Job and she could not understand why that should be. After all, he was the man who had saved her life and brought love and passion. But was he also not the catalyst? Had he not loaned Jack money would Jack have stolen from his clients and from her? If Job had not given him the funds, he might have pulled himself together.

She left the table and wandered down the garden. It was pretty and at the very end the wonderful New Zealand Christmas tree, the pohutakawa, was in full bloom. The crimson blossom was thick and heavy. She so loved this country and yet it was here that her life had started to unwind. But that was not the fault of the place but of Jack.

Perhaps Jack had always done things behind her back. It could be that there were two Jacks and she had been too blinded by loyalty to see it. It was not their coming here that had changed him, although he probably used that as an excuse.

But to offer the policy to clear his debts, a policy she had had no idea he had – and one, she was quick to remember, that was not found amongst his things – was too terrible to contemplate.

Had Jack expected them to collect and the only way they could collect would be by killing her? Was that what some-one was trying to do now?

Job had joined her, walking by her side but with a person distance between them.

'Whoever they are, they aren't very professional,' she said cynically.

'Or have you just been lucky? People arriving to save you – the farmer in Wales, me the night of the fire. I think they are very professional.'

'Who are they?' She was not really asking him but he answered anyway.

'That's what we need to find out. Perhaps it isn't they but whom.'

She turned to look at him. 'What do you mean?'

'It could be just one person. Someone he owed money to after me, after them. But it doesn't make sense. He sold the boat . . .'

'Did he give you that money?' There was an accusation in the question that even she did not much like.

'If he had I would have told you. I got nothing from Jack, or rather' – he shrugged – 'I got the rent he owed me and that came from you.'

'So there had to be someone else. I mean someone that he gave the boat money to.'

'Unless he spent that as well, although I can't see how. I put word out on him.'

'Job?' She turned to look up at him, fear in her eyes.

'Not that kind of word. I had a word with the people he gambled with. He could not get a game in Auckland, no matter what money he had.'

'You're sure? Because if that happened, how did he rack up even more debt.'

'Maybe he didn't do that. It could be that he intended to clear out, to leave you and go somewhere else.'

She pondered on that some long while. They reached his car but she did not pull open the passenger door, instead she turned. He was closer to her than she realized and they collided. He stepped back from her as if she had stung him. Oh, Job, she thought miserably, do I repulse you that much?

'Listen to me, Job. You mustn't say that to the police. I mean about your preventing him from gambling.'

'I want to be honest, Bron. That is what they need so they can look for who is doing this.'

202

'No, it won't make that much difference. If you say that, don't you see, if you say there was no one else, that you even *think* that there was no one else, then the only one with a motive to murder Jack is you.'

Job was silent for a long while. 'I don't give a damn what they think, just so long as you don't think I had anything to do with Jack's murder.'

'I don't think that. I've never thought that.'

'I thought you might have done. That day at the boat . . . I felt sure that was what you thought.'

'Well, I never did think that. It was like I said, they . . . the police . . . made me feel dirty and ashamed. That was what the matter was. People were gossiping about us too.' She shrugged. 'But that didn't stop even when I . . . when I called us off, it didn't make any difference.'

'I'm glad to hear that, Bron. You have to know I've done some things that I am not proud of, Bron, but I never hurt anyone. I am not into violence. I want you to believe that.'

'I do, Job, but the police might not see it that way.'

'Look, if I don't tell them, they might start looking around the gambling set, which is eating into the time they should be looking elsewhere. I think . . .'

'What?' she asked in the wake of his hesitation.

'I have a feeling there's something we are missing. Have you any idea what else Jack could have been involved with?'

'I did not think he was involved with anything. After all, I'm the one that didn't even know he had been fired from his job.'

'Yeah, I know. But was there anything else about him?'

'Apart from the drinking, nothing comes to mind.'

'Law wise, could he have been helping anyone in that field?'

'He was a property solicitor, Job. He never touched the

criminal side of the law. It wasn't his thing at all. All he did was property, wills, probate, that kind of thing. Never criminal work, ever.'

'What about forgery? He could have done something like that. Doctored a will. Is that possible?'

She was doubtful. 'I suppose so but his boss would know what work he carried out. You could mention that to the police or ask him.'

'That's something worth pursuing. See, there are things we don't know about. We have to give the police everything. I just don't want you getting hurt again . . .'

'I'm not keen on that myself!' She smiled up at him. 'We are friends now, aren't we, Job?'

'Sure,' he said. 'Let's get back. Ruthie will wonder where we got to.'

But Bron knew Ruthie would not care, if they were together, she and Job, then Ruthie would be very happy. It was a shame but what Ruthie wanted would never happen. She had blown it and it was too late to claw anything back.

When they turned into Ruthie's, Bron saw lots of people moving about the ruins of her house.

'Job, what's going on?' She clutched her throat in panic. Job smiled.

'There you go, they're clearing everything away.'

'What?'

'Your neighbours, the town's folk, said they'd come and do it. All I had to do was get you out of the way.'

'Oh.' She felt tears burn her eyes. She had been feeling resentful of the town's folk, suspecting they thought she had something to do with Jack's murder, and yet here they were, doing a filthy job for her. Leaving the car, she sped across the grass. Ruthie was supervizing with Adam. They, and the other folk, were filthy dirty.

'You people!' Bron said and then she burst into tears.

She was lost in a sea of hugs. She recalled much later the scent of smoke and charred wood. It did not matter, though; she welcomed the embrace. She realized that after all she did belong.

'I am going to rebuild,' she announced. 'I am not going to let the buggers grind me down.'

'Good for you!' someone cried. 'And we will help – must be some old photos of this place somewhere. You could design it just as it was!'

'That's what I'll do. This is my home, this was my house – it loved me, I know that now. I'm not going to let anyone frighten me away. This is where I belong.'

She thought to herself, I am jobless, I have no home. I owe the man I love a lot of money. He doesn't love me any more. My life has been turned upside-down and last and by no means least, my husband was murdered and someone tried to murder me. Yet she had inside her a tremendous lightness. These people had by their actions raised her spirits. They had, in fact, set her free. She could be strong again.

CHAPTER TWELVE

Job ran through the tall trees, leaping over broken branches like a young gazelle. He knew every twist and turn in the forest. It was his forest, the place where he belonged. His secret kingdom.

Of course it was not *that* secret. His Maori family knew precisely where he had his house. But the majority of people did not. It was the place he came to escape. To replenish himself. He bathed in the waters of the Pacific; he ran through the trees, he pounded along the beach. Somedays he just went to Cape Reingo and felt a spirit move through him. He could lose himself here. One day he would bring Bron to this magic kingdom but not yet. She was not ready and he was not ready to share it with her. The trust was not there yet; she said it was but he sensed a kernel of doubt. He did not blame her. She had been through so much that in some ways she was right to be suspicious of everyone and him in particular.

As he emerged into a clearing he saw an offroad vehicle outside his house. He backed up, hiding behind a tall tree. For a long while he observed the car. No one was sitting in the driving or passenger seat. It was not a vehicle he knew but he could not be certain as he could not see the number plate.

He went closer. The vehicle did not belong to any member of his family and no one else knew where this place was. There was only one thing this meant and it was a capital T'd trouble.

Softly, he crossed the ground; he moved swiftly and quietly, darting from tree to tree until he grew close to the house. He went to the back and, bending ran to the window.

Crouching down he peered through the wide expanse. He had left the door unlocked – he always did – and now it was open. Someone was sitting on the porch. He could see a thigh, but their back was obscured because the chair they were using was to the left of the door out on the veranda.

Surprise would give him advantage. He crawled towards the back door and, raising his hand turned the knob. The door did not even creak. As quietly and as swiftly as a snake, he moved through the entrance, crawling towards the door, and only as he neared it did he stand, flexing his hands, and then in a loud voice say, 'What do you want?'

The leg jerked. The person stood. There had been a little gasp of surprise and then the door filled with a presence. He rocked back on his heels. His advantage left him. He was more surprised than he had ever thought it possible to be.

'What the hell. . . ?' he said.

She was more beautiful than he remembered and certainly more sensual. The long blonde hair was loose and rippled over her round, rather deliciously plump shoulders. Her white off-the-shoulder sweater clung to her, and she wore it outside her short, tight skirt; her waist was clinched in with a tan leather thick belt, the surface spotted with brass studs. It was a more revealing and tantalizing outfit than she had ever worn before. Wow, his maleness thought, what had happened to *her*? Gone was the rather prim girl with the thick blonde plait, in her place this sensuous, confident beauty.

'Well, Job, don't you have anything to say to me?'

'What are you doing here? And more importantly how did you find this place?'

'I hope you are not going to be mad at me?' she whispered girlishly. 'I mean, I deserve some credit, right? For finding this place.' She smiled. 'It's no secret, Job, I followed you once a long time ago.'

He was incredulous. This woman was unbelievable! '*You* followed me. *You*?'

'Job, there is much more to me than meets the eye.'

'That I am beginning to realize.' He shook his head. 'I can't believe I didn't spot you. I'm so careful.'

'It was dark.'

'Dark? You followed me in the dark, through the forest. I can't believe that.'

'Believe me, Job. How else do you think I found you? I mean, you know damn well Ruthie wouldn't tell me where you hung out. You would never tell me, and dear sweet Bron, well, you never told her, or did you?'

'I didn't as it happens.'

'Can I come inside? Will you offer me tea, or . . .' She took a deep breath, her eyes widening. 'Anything?'

'I have tea and coffee or Coca-Cola. I don't keep booze up here.'

'Tea would be lovely.'

'Come in then.'

He was glad of the diversion; his mind was spinning. Marged had followed him and he had not been aware of it.

What was going on, with him and with her? How could she have done that, that simpering, rather dreamy but deep girl? A British city girl had trailed him in a car and then somehow manoeuvred on foot around the track without him knowing about it. He could not believe it. Something smelt rotten. But how else could she have got here?

The kettle whistling brought him out of his reverie. He was going to play it close to his chest. She was up to something and he intended to find out what it was.

After making the tea, he turned to her once more. She was sitting on the settee, her legs crossed at the knee, showing a great deal of thigh. What had happened to that modest girl he had first met? She had always worn simple clothes, and her hair – that glorious blonde mane – that had always been kept under control.

'Have you seen anything of Bron?' He put down the tea things on the occasional table.

'I'll pour,' she said. He let her take control. Once she had poured the tea, she turned her enormous eyes on him. Her lashes had been dyed: they were very black. It should have looked odd but it didn't. The black emphasized the unusual topaz colour of her iris.

'What happened? The house isn't there. I got a shock.' She put her hand to her heart. 'I thought I'd go and ask Ruthie but you know . . .' She shrugged. 'Ruthie never liked me. I thought she would not tell me.'

'Anyone in town could have told you. The house burned down.'

'Oh my God, and Bron?' Her face flushed. She did not pale as if in shock but looked as if she were excited.

'Bron's OK. She's living in town. She plans to rebuild. Bron has a lot of guts; she won't let it finish her.'

'How did it happen?'

209

'It was done deliberately.'

'No.'

'Oh yes, Marged. Someone tried to kill her . . . again.'

'That's terrible.' Insincerity oozed from her. She did not even try to be concerned. He supposed that was honest but he started to loathe her.

'Poor Bron, she's lost so much. She really loved that house.'

'Yes, she did.'

'I'll bet she was more upset about the house than she was about Jack.'

She had the gall to smile after she had said it. He stared at her, keeping his features controlled.

'Bron never liked me and, truthfully, I never liked her.'

'Then why did you come out here?'

She shrugged again, lifted her teaspoon and, putting it into her cup, stirred the liquid gently. When she had done, she took up the spoon and licked it.

'I wanted to get away. This is about as far as I could get. You know I had had a terrible time,' she lisped.

'Yes I do, Marged, and I felt very sorry because of it. Bron was good to you but you hit her, didn't you?'

Her eyes flashed him a look, and she pursed her lips. 'I did not hit Bron. I don't know why you would say that I did.'

'She told me you did.'

'And of course you believed her?' She sighed. 'She was very nasty to me after you left. Accused me of damaging the floor, then she had the gall to warn me off you. I mean, does she own you?' Her lashes fluttered. 'I wouldn't have thought anyone owned you, Job.'

'No one does, least of all Bron.' He felt something moving over him, a vague perception. All his nerve ends were

210

standing upright. He was like a cat and someone had brushed his fur the wrong way. That was exactly how he felt. But like a cat he could be very crafty too.

'We had a fling, that was all.'

'Oh Job!' she giggled. 'That was mean of you. I mean, she had to have been feeling so vulnerable.' She stood, smoothed down her skirt and crossed to him. When she was in touching distance, she placed her hands on his shoulders and slowly lowered herself on to his lap. He bit on the exclamation. 'She isn't your type, Job. You found that out, eh?'

'Sure,' he murmured. 'She knew that. It was just one of those things.'

'Wham bam and thank you, ma'am. I was sure that Bron never went in for that kind of thing. There was never anyone in her life but Jack, you know.'

'I didn't know. It didn't seem that way to me.'

'Oh, really.' She smoothed her hands over the back of his head, pausing to loosen the leather thong that tied it back. 'I am positive, but I suppose I could be wrong.' She looked down at him. 'You are a beautiful man, you know, Job. I never met anyone quite like you.'

'I'm not special.'

'Oh, you are.' She bent her head. Her lips when they fastened on his tasted like sweet, hot cherries. Her hand she slid down his body until she found the rim of his T-shirt, then she slid the hand inside, moving over his skin with sensual movements.

'What are you doing?' he asked, slowly extricating himself from her kiss.

'You, I hope, Job, mm?'

He was about to say, No, you won't. He wanted to keep her happy but not *that* happy. All he wanted was to get her to tell him things. He was filled with apprehension about her now. His instincts were on overdrive but no matter what he wanted, he was not prepared to go that far! However, he was saved by a strangled sound. Marged's whole body started, and she left his knee like a jack leaving its box.

A man stood in the doorway. Now, Job thought, that is one good looking guy. Far better looking than him. He could have been in the films or gracing a poster. Small, slender, dark, almost Spanish-looking.

'What are you doing?' Job realized he had more authority to ask the question but he bit on the words. He watched one and then the other, feeling the tension between them. His highly tuned antenna told him he was in trouble.

'I'm just trying to pump him,' she said, and there was in her voice a sliver of fear that Job picked up on. Gone was the seductive creature of moments ago. Now she was as tense as a bow string.

'I hope you weren't going to shag him.'

'Don't be ridiculous.' She laughed nervously.

'You know what happens when you do that? I get angry.'

'Don't be silly, darling.' She sidled up to him, smoothing a hand over his sweater.

'You don't think I'd want him after she's had him all over her.'

'There is that but then there was the other—'

'That couldn't be helped. You know that I had to get—'

'Shut it,' he said. 'Walls have ears.'

'There's no one for miles around.'

Job had had enough. He stood, glad that he dwarfed them both.

'Sit down.'

'Get out,' Job said, 'both of you, before I throw you out.'

'I don't think you'll do that,' the man said, and then from his pocket he drew a gun. It was small, the sort of thing a woman would carry, but Job was no fool and knew that even a small revolver could do a lot of damage, especially if he knew how to use it.

'OK' he said, lowering himself back into the chair. 'Just what do you want?'

Bron turned off the cooker. She checked her watch. It was turned eight and still no sign of Ruthie. Adam was working away and she had thought it would be a nice idea to have Ruthie for dinner.

Picking up the telephone, she rang Ruthie's number but it just continued to ring out. Then she tried Ruthie's mobile number. That went to voicemail.

It was not like Ruthie to just not answer; even if she was on her way she would not have switched off her mobile. She had said she would walk. That was definite. Her words came winging into Bron's mind. 'I'll walk then we can share a bottle of *vino collapso!*'

'Sounds like a plan,' Bron said. She felt happy they were friends again. Her friendship with Ruthie, she realized, was very important to her. Just like her friendship with Job. Only she admitted she wanted more than friendship with Job. She longed for what she had thrown away. Knowing that she could never have it, she would settle for his friendship, painful as that was.

Deciding it was definitely not like Ruthie, Bron set off for her home. She took the car – it was only a ten minute walk but she did not want to waste time. If Ruthie had fallen or hurt herself . . . What had happened to her? If things did not go to plan, she always looked on the dark side now. This pessimism was really getting to her, yet, she counselled

213

herself, who could blame her with all that happened. But Ruthie was one of those prompt people.

She passed no one on the way, it was that time when everyone was home eating. Ruthie's house, thank God, stood as firm as it had for nigh on fifty years. The beautiful white painted colonial home was a reminder of her own home and how happy she had been there. I will get there again, she vowed to herself. It will happen – one day soon.

'Ruthie!' she called from the veranda even before she reached the front door. The front door was not locked. Nothing unusual in that. She pushed it open and called, hearing her voice dancing through the silence.

Cautiously, she stepped inside after kicking off her shoes. The wooden boards were warm against the soles of her feet, so warm in fact that her feet were sticking to the wood.

The silence more or less told her that Ruthie was not home. Ruthie always had music playing; she loved music with a passion. Reluctant to leave, Bron went deeper into the house, calling her friend's name as she did.

The dining-room doors were closed but she peered in. Nothing was amiss there. She went through to the sitting room.

If houses smiled, this room smiled. It was so comfortable and friendly, filled with books and carvings, a piano in one corner, the settee huge and comfortable. She called again and then paused to listen. There was a sound – a soft keening noise. 'Ruthie!' Without caution she darted across the floor to the kitchen, pushed open the door and saw Ruthie. There was blood but she was sitting up, trussed like a chicken, thick tape over her mouth.

'My God!' Bron dashed across the kitchen. Falling to her knees, she gently pulled the tape from Ruthie's mouth. A huge purple bruise was forming on her cheekbone and the blood was coming from her nose.

'Job, they've gone for Job . . .'

'Who has?'

Ruthie was struggling to get up. Bron tried to ease her back down but the woman insisted they had to go. Bron had to drive. They had to protect Job.

'It's her, it was her all along!' Ruthie was hysterical. 'I knew she was strange, I felt it—'

'You can't mean Marged?'

Ruthie was on her feet. 'Come on, help me to the car. You'll have to drive. Out towards Ninety Mile Beach then I'll show you the way . . .'

Bron felt confused. Unable for the moment to act, she just stood and stared at Ruthie, watching as the pain kicked in on her friend, causing her to shake uncontrollably.

'You can't go. We'll have to call the police.'

'*No police*. Not yet. He won't want the police tramping over his place. Come on . . .'

'You're in shock, you can't go yet—'

'I'm going. If I have to go on my own I will! I'm telling you Job's in danger. She wants to get him now!'

'I'm coming with you but you have to have something, Ruthie. You could pass out.'

'Get me a brandy, that'll have to do.'

Ruthie could hardly walk. Carrying the bottle of brandy and knowing all the time it was the wrong thing to give her to drink, Bron nevertheless helped her into her car. It was a four-wheel drive, better for travelling up north, if they had to go off the track. Ruthie sat with her head back on the rest, holding a pack at her nose. Bron drove as fast as she could. She had had the forethought to bring the icepack and it had almost stopped the bleeding.

Words rattled out of Ruthie. How she had come home from the dairy to find Marged in the house. At first she had been friendly, asking where Bron had gone. Then when Ruthie wouldn't tell her where her cousin was, or where Job was, she had got heavy. Ruthie could handle her, then the man came.

'What man?'

'I never saw him before. A little guy, not big like Job, but a born thug.'

'I wonder if she got in with the people Jack was in deep with.'

'I don't know. He wasn't a New Zealander, though. He was English.'

'English? Are you sure?'

'Positive. He spoke a little like you. Faint accent – north country.'

Images flashed into and just as quickly out of Bron's mind. Something was on the brink of her memory but the harder she thought about it the more it went away.

'I'm so sorry!' Ruthie sobbed suddenly. 'I didn't want to dob about where Job was but I couldn't stop myself.'

'You mustn't blame yourself. If they hurt you . . .'

'He really hurt me.' Ruthie's hand trembled as she obviously relived the memory. 'He knew how to hurt without it showing. He said he would rip off my nails. I couldn't stand it; I knew he would do it. God forgive me.'

'Job wouldn't want you to suffer like that, Ruthie. Oh, Ruthie, it's me that should be sorry, it's my entire fault. I can't understand what has happened to her.'

'She's crazy, Bron, really crazy, and he isn't any better.'

It was growing dark now, and the huge trees dominated each side of the road. Ruthie almost missed the track where they turned off – it would be barely discernible during the day but at night it was well hidden.

As they hit the track that went through the trees, there was another turn and this time no track. Bron was afraid she would hit a tree and slowed down, thankful they had taken the four-wheel drive.

'What is this place?'

'It's where he lives. I don't ask. Things used to go on up here, not with Job, he was not into that but . . .' Ruthie shrugged.

'What kind of things?'

'Growing weed, that sort of thing.'

'Oh.' I've come a long way, Bron thought. I am not even shocked and it seems mild in comparison to what my cousin is up to.

'Stop,' Ruthie whispered urgently. Through the trees a sliver of light cut into the darkness. Bron did as she was told, cutting the engine right away.

'If they are there do you think they heard?'

'Could've done. Look, I'm going to go over there, Ruthie. I want you to stay here. Promise me you'll do that.'

'What can you do?'

'You'd be surprised. She's not getting away with this, Ruthie.'

'But what about the thug?'

'I'll have to take care of him first.'

I'm scared, she thought, I really am so afraid. Before leaving she had taken the jack out of the back of the car. It rested in her hand; she kept a firm grip on it.

There was no sound from the cabin. Bending, she peered in through the window. Job was there. He was sitting in a chair but he was not tied up. She saw Marged first, standing hands on hips, looking different somehow. Standing

217

next to her was a man. He was wearing jeans and a T-shirt. He was as tall as Marged but slim in a wiry, fit kind of way. He had an arm outstretched and he was holding something but she could not see what since he had his back to her.

The element of surprise. That was what happened in the movies but did it work in real life? There was nothing else for it. Standing, she went to the door and slowly turned the door knob, which thankfully did not make a sound. She pushed the door a little way open, peering inside. Job was facing her. She was sure he saw her but his face remained impassive.

With a quick movement she slammed back the door with her foot, at the same time hurling the jack. It hit its target, straight into the man's shoulder. The force of it sent him forward. Job did the rest.

How stupid, Bron thought ridiculously, not to tie him up. Job's leg went right up between the man's legs and he gasped in agony, falling to his knees. Something shot out of his hand.

Marged turned around, and instead of going for whatever had flown out of the man's hand, she snarled like a wild, uncontrolled animal and with arms up, hands bent like claws, she leapt towards Bron. With more alacrity than she knew she possessed, Bron leapt to one side and Marged lost balance. Before she could recover, Job was on to her, twisting her arm around her back. He had a gun in one hand, aimed at the man who was still in pain, writhing on the floor.

Job, still holding on to a squirming, screaming Marged, barked out a telephone number for Bron to dial. She thought it the police and told them to hurry, as he had dictated, to Job Tepi's house.

Only it wasn't the police, it was members of his family.

218

About ten of them. They were huge men, built like rugby players.

'We can take these in. No need for the police to come up here,' Job bit out angrily when she asked if the police would be coming.

The men tied up the man and helped Job tie Marged down. She was still squirming and screaming obscenities.

'Shall I knock her out?' one of the men asked. Bron muttered, 'no, don't hurt her,' but it was Job they listened to. 'We can't do that, but we can do this,' he said. He took up a cloth and made a gag for around her mouth. 'Now, Marged, if you promise to shut up I'll take it off you,' but her answer was to kick out at him.

'Wild cat,' one of the men said.

'You could say that,' Job muttered.

CHAPTER THIRTEEN

DENIS had not gone away, at least not permanently. He had grown sick of his wife's mother and who could blame him. But Marged had known where he was, and they had communicated secretly. Marged had a phone that had a text facility. Her mother had not known about it.

In the end she had lost it with her mother one day, hitting her across the back of the head with a heavy weight. Denis had thought up the burglary idea. He had come running to arrange things after she called him. They were free, only Marged was not content. She wanted more from life. The money was not enough.

Her getting away with it had given her confidence but it had also pushed Marged over the edge. She needed Denis. He would always clean things up for her. She knew that as sure as anything, he was crazy about her.

Marged never said anything to the police; she confessed to nothing. It was Denis who confessed it all. But she had told her psychiatrist things that had helped the police put one or two unexplained matters to rest.

She had told him that she had wanted what her cousin had, but more than that, she had wanted Job Tepi too. However, she was stuck with Denis and somehow had to rid herself of him after he had done her bidding. She had not thought how she would do that. There was a chance Job could help in that department. She believed Job walked a fine line where law and order was concerned.

It did not worry her, she said, because she knew that Job would know what to do. It was amazing, Bron thought, that she imagined that Job would do something bad like get rid of Denis. She did not know Job at all. She thought he was someone he was not.

It was a senior policeman who explained everything to Bron. Not, thankfully, Sergeant Cartwright who mysteriously, had been kept out of the picture. Probably, she thought, Job's influence.

There was an insurance policy on her mother, and the sale of the house and shop had given Marged money. The trip to New Zealand had meant to be a stop-over on a round-the-world holiday. Her intention had been to boast to her cousin about the money she had. However, when she saw what Bron had, she had become even more irrational. When she met Job Tepi she had become obsessed with him.

Denis did not know why Marged had told Jack she had money. It catapulted Jack into explaining to her his money problems. Promising to lend Jack money, she took the insurance policy as collateral but she had no intention of giving Jack anything. He came on to her and she thought it would be fun to sleep with her cousin's husband. She knew that Jack did not care about Bron because he had told her. He had said he was ready to dump Bron but he needed the house money before doing so. However, she did not know that Bron also had doubts about her feelings for Jack. She still believed that Bron was in love with him. She felt she was taking something that Bron treasured. That was something she liked to do.

Catching her with Jack, Denis had beaten the man up. Jack had fallen and cracked his head. They both decided to get rid of his body. It would be the safest thing to do. Another robbery would bring suspicion on her head. If the New Zealand police put two and two together they could easily make four.

Dangling the insurance policy as bait, Marged persuaded Denis to kill Bron, only he failed with both attempts. Even more deranged by this time, she said she wanted to have him kill Job Tepi, only Denis suspected, seeing how she acted towards Tepi, that what she hoped for was that Tepi would overcome Denis.

'She really went for that bloke,' Denis said to the police. 'I held a gun on him and she was going on and on about me not doing him. She wouldn't shut up about it; we would have been out of there if only she had shut up. As it was, it was she who caused everything to go wrong. I never guessed she wanted him that bad.'

'I never knew she was as bad as that,' Bron whispered. 'That she hated me that much.' She was sitting in the police station. The inspector was kind and considerate in his telling her what happened. There were no accusations against Job or her. No snide comments about their relationship.

'She did but she also has serious psychological problems.'

'But if she had been brought up differently . . .'

'Don't worry about it, Mrs Mellor. None of it is your fault.

Bron felt sadder than she thought it possible, for Marged. She tried to go and see her but her cousin refused her visit. She told Ruthie, 'She couldn't help it.'

Ruthie, deciding it was best not to comment, merely went

and hugged Bron to her.

'You did your best, honey, so don't worry about it. You have to get on with your own life now. You deserve to have some fun.'

She took up the paperwork again. It would have caused a smile had she not been so miserable, because the money had come through for Jack's death. How ironic was that? She had the money that he had wanted to get from her own death. She could pay back Job Tepi, and only then would she be free. He would argue about it, she knew that, but she was stubborn too and that was something he had to realize. There was no way she was going to let him refuse a payment for Jack's debts.

Her beautiful house would soon be ready to move into. She had no fear of going back there. The deranged and sad girl had gone away. No one else wanted to harm her. After all, who was she? Just an ordinary woman.

The future would be different. School had asked her to go back but she had turned them down. She was thinking about going into business with Job. Running sailing trips for visitors and sailing lessons for those wishing to learn. She had all the necessary certificates; it would not be a problem. Job's hotels would be a good recruiting ground for clients.

Looking at her reflection, she noticed that the trauma had caused her to lose quite a lot of weight. Her collar bones stood out very clearly. She toyed with the idea of wearing a scarf then dismissed it as vanity. Once things settled down she would put the weight back on and not look so gaunt. She pinned on the sash of the MacLennan clan. Ruthie had given it to her for Christmas. It was a beautiful dark tartan.

There was lightness in her step as she walked towards

Ruthie's house. She passed people in the street and they stopped to say hello. Mr Connor was closing up the dairy for the night and he shouted a cheery good night. Everything was as it was. It was going to be OK now.

As she neared the garden she heard the sound of a reel and smiled to herself. Burns Night was in full swing.

Opening the gate, she stepped into the garden. Job was there. Seeing her, he came towards her.

'You look lovely,' he said, and he bent his head to kiss her cheek. She gazed up at him. 'Can't you do better than that?' she asked boldly. She knew she was going to have to do the pursuing now. It was all going to be down to her and she was not going to let pride get in her way. Not ever again.

'Sure,' but it was half a question and half a promise. After a moment's hesitation, he bent and kissed her fully on the lips. She parted hers for him, letting him see that if he wanted, then it was all right again.

When he let her go, he took her hand. He looked up at the sky, and she followed his gaze, watching as the clouds, as if by magic, rolled on.

There was a glimpse of a dark red glow in the sky.

'The clouds are breaking,' she said.

'It will be a lovely today tomorrow,' he promised.